A Civil Death

A VIKING NOVEL
OF
MYSTERY
AND
SUSPENSE

BY JOHN WILLIAM CORRINGTON AND JOYCE H. CORRINGTON

So Small a Carnival
A Project Named Desire

ALSO BY JOHN WILLIAM CORRINGTON

POETRY
Where We Are
Mr. Clean and Other Poems
The Anatomy of Love
Lines to the South

FICTION
And Wait for the Night
The Upper Hand
The Lonesome Traveller and Other Stories
The Bombardier
The Actes and Monuments
The Southern Reporter
Shad Sentell

EDITED WITH MILLER WILLIAMS
Southern Writing in the Sixties: Fiction
Southern Writing in the Sixties: Poetry

A Civil Death

John William Corrington
Joyce H. Corrington

Viking

VIKING
Viking Penguin Inc., 40 West 23rd Street,
New York, New York 10010, U.S.A.
Penguin Books Ltd, 27 Wrights Lane,
London, W8 5TZ
(Publishing & Editorial) and Harmondsworth,
Middlesex, England (Distribution & Warehouse)
Penguin Books Australia Ltd, Ringwood,
Victoria, Australia
Penguin Books Canada Limited, 2801 John Street,
Markham, Ontario, Canada L3R 1B4
Penguin Books (N.Z.) Ltd, 182–190 Wairau Road,
Auckland 10, New Zealand

First published in 1987 by Viking Penguin Inc.
Published simultaneously in Canada

LIBRARY OF CONGRESS CATALOGING IN PUBLICATION DATA
Corrington, John William.
A civil death.
I. Corrington, Joyce H.   II. Title.
PS3553.07C58   1987   813'.54   86-40491
ISBN 0-670-81490-3

Printed in the United States of America by
Arcata Graphics, Fairfield, Pennsylvania
Set in Palatino
Designed by Lucy Albanese

A. M. D. G.
And for Paddy

He begins to leave who begins to love.
  Many the leaving who know it not,
for the feet of those leaving are
  affections of the heart:
and yet they are leaving Babylon.

—AUGUSTINE,
  Enarrationes in
  Psalmos 64.2

A Civil Death

CHAPTER
1

It was still cold and dark when Wes dropped me off at the entrance to St. Louis Cemetery. As he drove away in my car to find a parking space along the crumbling brick wall, I pulled my fur tight around my neck and walked through the wrought-iron gate just as the elderly keeper opened it.

—Morning, ma'am, he said softly. —Can I help you with them flowers?

—Good morning, I said. —No, thank you. I can manage.

I walked down a narrow lane between mausoleums, each one built like a classical temple standing on its own plot of land. Some were of marble, some of granite. A few of the very old tombs were built of brick covered over with plaster. Around and between them were trees—magnolias, live oaks—as old as the cemetery itself—and St. Louis Cemetery is older than America.

—It's gonna be a bright morning, the old keeper

called after me as he looked out toward the east. —A nice bright morning for the souls.

I nodded. The sky above was cloudless, stars beginning to fade as midnight blue lightened to gray. It was chill for so early in November. The chill of the grave, I remember thinking.

As the light grew, I could make out names on the tombs I passed. Duplessis, Couvillon, Lanier, Benedetto. I realized how many of the families represented there had been intertwined with mine over the years. Margaret Duplessis had been queen of the Carnival Krewe of Pandora the year after me. Father James Couvillon had once been assistant pastor of our parish and was now a missionary priest somewhere in Central America. Dick Lanier had been our family doctor for as long as I could remember. I had gone to Newcomb College at Tulane with Sarah and Anne Benedetto. Here in these cold temples were their people, the generations left behind, static now, speechless, taking part in our lives only through memory—and the moment of ritual we paid them on All Souls' Day.

Then I reached the place I was seeking.

It was not quite like the others. The tomb was larger and stood apart at an intersection of two lanes wider than most. Instead of the usual rectangle it was round, a small copy of the temple of Artemis at Ephesus—almost identical to the classical structure atop the Hibernia Bank Building in downtown New Orleans. On the marble steps leading up to the sealed door, my family name was carved.

LEMOYNE

Behind the bronze door wrought with whorls of laurel, sorrowing angels, and all the ordinary emblems of loss and devotion lay my father and mother, my grandfather and grandmother Lemoyne, and the anonymous bones of generations of the family who had been gathered there long ago from down in the parishes by Auguste Lemoyne, my grandfather, when he had come into enough money through marriage to build his own family's temple in the city of the dead.

That's what my grandfather had called St. Louis Cemetery. He hadn't invented the name. It was common in New Orleans, applied to all the cemeteries in town. There is a human community, my grandfather told me when I was a little girl and scarcely understood him. It consists of the living, the dead, and the yet unborn. We are all members of it together. We should cherish one another. We should be kind, remember, look forward.

I felt tears in my eyes as I emptied out last week's flowers from the stone urns set on either side of the sealed tomb. The sun had risen, and its first rays struck the weathered door in front of me. I almost raised my hand as if to knock, to seek early entry into that house where all my people were, where no one lived.

—Cold as a bear's ass out there, Denise, I heard Wes say behind me.

As always, his presence warmed me. I moved into the circle of his arms and kissed him. He smelled of tobacco and leather—earthy things. His lopsided smile said there may be a lot of serious matters in this world, but I haven't seen many, and the ones I have seen can all be reduced to irony and laughter. If you're brave enough.

Wes looked at the Lemoyne tomb, leaning left and right, squinting, shaking his head.

—New Orleanians have got to be the only people in the world who spend more on their graves than they do on their houses.

—The Egyptians, I answered.

—Currently living, I mean. I guess you can call what youall do living.

John Wesley Colvin of Shreveport, Caddo Parish, Louisiana, has no love for my city. A newspaperman, veteran of police beats all over the state, he had intended to settle only for a while at the *New Orleans Item*, waiting for the big story that would mean advancement to a New York or Chicago paper. When the story had finally come, he buried the best chance he'd ever get— for love of me.

It would be easy enough to say I love him because he had surely saved my sanity, possibly my life. Or to say that when my grandfather was murdered, Wes had pressed on, scraping and probing, digging and delving, almost losing his own life, until he found out why—then kept those dark reasons to himself. But there's much more than that. There's the smile, and a certain driving, unpredictable intensity that lies behind it. A vital self-certainty that can be irritating and annoying and wrongheaded and utterly lovable. Like most people from north Louisiana, Wes is a barbarian. He never complains, never explains. When he decides to get something done, it gets done.

Just then, he had in mind to get me out of the cemetery and to some place for breakfast where liquor was served—a Mimosa for me, a Bloody Mary with extra Tabasco for Wes. There are numerous such places all over New Orleans. Open at any hour of the day or night.

I made the sign of the cross and thought with love of my mother—and especially of my grandfather. Grand-père would have liked Wes. He hadn't been a barbarian at all, but he would have smiled to think that an un-kempt young reporter from Caddo Parish had evened the score for him. Then I said a very brief, very formal prayer for my father. Not because I wanted to. Because it was my duty.

Wes and I were about to start walking back down the narrow lane toward the entrance when I saw a woman, carrying a wreath of flowers, pause before the tomb next to the Lemoynes'. For a moment, I didn't recognize her. She was quite tall, slender, dressed in slacks and a ragged old sweater that perhaps had once been red but was now a spiritless brown. She wore sunglasses and a drab scarf over her hair, and I might have turned away and left if I hadn't seen a whisp of it pulled forward, lying across her forehead bright as spun gold.

—Madeline? I said, not sure I could believe my eyes.

She turned from fixing her wreath to the door of the tomb and seemed to study me for a moment, as if she were deciding whether she knew me. Then she tried to smile.

—Denise, she murmured, and opened her arms to me.

Madeline Holman St. Juste was my godmother. Her father, Henry Holman, publisher of the *New Orleans Item*, my godfather. Though we were not related by blood, Madeline had been something of a mother to me after my own had died. Even more, we had been the best of friends as I grew up. I crossed the few steps between us quickly and brushed her cold cheek with my lips as we embraced.

As I pulled back, I must have looked at her curiously. She always dressed with quiet elegance, but today she looked disheveled. I had never seen her like this before. Behind sunglasses, her eyes were hollow. Her face was pale, almost chalky. I wondered if she were ill.

She turned away from my glance and looked again at the door of the Holman mausoleum where her own mother had been buried just a few months ago after years of illness.

—It doesn't seem so bad on a day like this, does it? she said with forced brightness. —Almost like . . . a winter place.

—You're still feeling awful about your mother, aren't you?

She nodded. —Yes. Just as if I hadn't watched her dying since I was in college.

—I'm sorry I haven't been by since the funeral. I've started work as an assistant in the district attorney's office.

—I heard. I was surprised. Almost as much as I was by your engagement.

Madeline glanced past me at Wes as she squirreled in her purse and came up with a platinum case. She offered me a cigarette. I shook my head and watched her hands shake as she tried several times to make her lighter strike fire.

—I know I look like shit, she said, drawing on the cigarette and blowing a cloud, like unintended incense, toward the Holman tomb. —But I'd like to meet your . . . fiancé.

I felt the smallest wrinkle of surprise. Madeline didn't ordinarily use that sort of language. She was a Newcomb lady, who graduated before Newcomb girls wore jeans, let their hair go natural, and assumed habits of speech that rivaled the Tulane football team. I turned to draw Wes into the conversation.

—This is Wesley Colvin. Wes, my godmother, Madeline Holman St. Juste. Uncle Henry's daughter.

Wes smiled and waited for Madeline to extend her hand. She didn't

—You're . . . at Daddy's paper, aren't you?

—Yes, ma'am.

She smiled back then, her light eyes cold as opals.

—Daddy says you're a brilliant writer, very clever, utterly ruthless—and obsessed with history.

Wes shook his head in feigned delight.

—I didn't know Henry felt that way about me, ma'am. Maybe I'll just hit him up for a raise.

Madeline laughed dryly. —Don't bother. I believe Daddy already has . . . something in mind for you.

Wes didn't blink. —I hope I live through it, he said.

Madeline turned back to me. It was obvious her little passage at arms with Wes hadn't been satisfactory. I could have warned her.

—I'm sure Wesley wouldn't mind if you walked back to my car with me, she said.

I glanced at Wes. He had his hands in his pockets, and a fresh unlit cigar in his mouth.

—Wes . . . ?

—Go right ahead, honey, he told me. —I'll look around a minute more. This place fascinates me. Maybe I'll do some interviews with the permanent residents.

Madeline shivered, and we began walking back toward the cemetery gate while children ran laughing and screaming past the silent tombs.

—Darling . . . we used to be so close. René and I thought of you as the daughter we never had. Have lunch with me tomorrow, will you?

—I'd love to, Madeline, but . . .

—What?

—Tomorrow I have some bail hearings in Judge Quintero's court . . .

I only saw her from the corner of my eye, but it seemed Madeline almost paused in her stride, stiff-

ened, as if I'd said something offensive. Was it the ref-
erence to my job as assistant district attorney? Madeline
was of that generation that didn't quite understand
why a woman of good family and means would choose
to work.

—But they shouldn't run past noon, I added, as if I
had something to apologize for.

We'd reached the cemetery gate by then. —Fine,
Madeline said. —Then I'll meet you there. Whenever
you're done, we'll find a nook somewhere. Division "I"
of Criminal Court?

—That's right, I told her. —We could run out to the
Caribbean Room at the Pontchartrain.

—That would be lovely. You see . . .

Her voice trailed off. Suddenly she looked much
older, a little frightened, more than a little unhappy.

—Madeline, what is it?

—I have to talk to . . . someone. It's private . . . and I
couldn't bear talking to anyone but you.

She put her arms around me quickly, gave me a
dry kiss, and headed down the sun-bright street toward her limousine. I saw a dark good-looking man
straighten from leaning against the fender. He opened
her door, closed it behind her, then got in and drove
away. I watched as the car's passage stirred dead
leaves heaped in the gutters into a brief spiraling moment of life, and wondered what had troubled Madeline so, what it was she wanted to discuss so urgently
with me over lunch.

Then Wes came up from behind me, kissed my neck.
I felt the familiar thrill of his touch and forgot Madeline
and her problems. We walked hand in hand up the
street toward my car.

I had come early to the cemetery so we'd have time
for breakfast at Brennan's or somewhere else in the

Quarter before we went to work, but things didn't
work out that way. As we headed downtown, the traffic on my police radio suddenly picked up. Wes and I
both listened.

—Uh, base, we got uh...hostage situation. Broad
Street. Schwegmann's Supermarket. Subject male Cau-
casian. No name. Shooting at armed off-duty Orleans
Parish deputy...female, Janna Donovan. Uh...what's
that? You're breaking up. No, no. She's okay. But female deputy shot subject male. Subject grabbed stock
clerk. Holed up in store. Wants somebody from D.A.'s
office...to talk a deal.

—Shit, Wes said. —On All Souls' Day?

—It's not far. I'll swing by, I told him.

When we reached Schwegmann's Giant Supermarket
on Broad, there were police cars everywhere. Traffic
had been rerouted, and most of the officers were leaning against cars, riot guns slung over the hoods and
trunks. It looked like a war zone. I put my district attorney's parking permit up on the dashboard near the
window and passed through the police line. Ahead a
car door opened, and I hit the brakes just in time to
avoid a smartly dressed black man as he stepped out of
the car. Captain Ralph "Rat" Trapp frowned and looked
down at us. Then he smiled.

—I thought you might be that outlaw's girlfriend
coming to get him out, he said.

—I keep company with another outlaw, I said, nodding at Wes.

They laughed and shook hands. Wes and Rat are the
best of friends.

—Here's what we got, Rat began. —You see that
sweet little blond morsel sitting in the back of my car?
That's Janna Donovan, Orleans Parish criminal deputy.

—Lord, Wes said admiringly. —Miss Louisiana with a .38 special.

—She never did that good, Rat said without a smile. —She was third runner-up.

—What happened? I asked.

—She was off duty, making groceries. She parked and started to get out of her car, and this ding-dong we got cornered took a shot at her.

I looked over at the supermarket building. It was old and immense, and the wide roof was used for parking. The ramp that led up to the parking area was empty now, except for an abandoned car or two standing with doors open. They'd been vacated in a hurry.

—Seems our lady deputy don't take to being shot at. She come around on this ass and popped him with her service revolver. She thinks she got meat. He cut and run downstairs.

Wes whistled. —You never can tell anymore . . .

—That's right, Rat went on. —So keep your pistol in your pocket and your gun in your pants.

—The shooter's still inside? I asked, determined not to laugh.

—Oh yeah. Couple of shots cleared the place out, and he grabbed some poor Vietnamese kid who was stocking the shelves. Got her in the receiving room. There's a steel door on the outside to prevent theft. If we have to go in for her, it'll be right down the aisles between the lettuce and the canned soup.

—You said "her"? Wes asked.

—That's right. Seems our shooter likes to do it to women.

—Why'd he shoot? Did he try to take the deputy's purse, pull her into a car, anything? I asked.

Rat shook his head, his eyes wandering over the building as he answered. —No, honey. Just cut loose and shot. My guess is he wanted the little lady dead. See, the shot he fired at Janna . . . he used a silencer.

Wes and I exchanged a look. I'd never heard of anyone using a silencer in a mugging or a stickup.

—My God, I said. —It was a hit?

—Well, what can I tell you?

Wes was looking more interested by the moment. —Maybe she put him away. Some punk who's mad at her.

—We gonna get that part squared away just as soon as I pull him out of there. That scumbag is gonna sound like a symphony orchestra. We're waiting for the D.A. to send us somebody to . . .

—I'm here, I said, feeling suddenly and definitely colder than the brisk north wind justified.

—Oh, no, Rat and Wes said, almost together.

—Please don't start the protective-male stuff with me. I'm here, I'm needed, and I'm going in.

—Goddamnit, Rat said, —there's two dozen assistant D.A.'s I'd as soon see blanked as not. You ain't any of 'em.

—Denise, Wes began, his expression serious, no trace of humor or irony in his eyes, —don't do it. They don't pay you enough.

I tried to make it light. —I know. But I keep taking their money. Let's do it.

—You know the last time I heard somebody say that? Wes asked. —Gary Gilmore. Just before they blew him away up in Utah.

They talked to the shooter on a bullhorn then, and I took a deep breath, pushed any reservations out of my mind, and walked through the wide front door of the supermarket.

Alone, inside the empty store, it was eerie. I found

myself seeing things in precise detail that I'd never noticed before. There were stacks and stacks of loss-leader B&M pork and beans, Northern toilet tissue, and Bartles & Jaymes wine cooler near the door, near a corral of shopping carts that seemed to be in even greater disarray than usual.

One of the cash registers at a checkout line was open, money and checks spilled out on the floor. Bags of groceries, half-sacked, had fallen and split and spilled their cargo in my way. The place was blindingly bright, dozens of overhead lights shining down on rank after rank, file after file of the ordinary things we use every day of our lives.

For the first time, I saw—really saw—the bright labels on tin cans and plastic sacks and pasteboard boxes. Names flared out at me. Kix, Pampers, Crosse & Blackwell, Old El Paso, Four Seasons. Things I'd picked out and tossed in my shopping cart hundreds of times and had never really seen.

Even though it was late fall, the air-conditioning was running. I could hear it in the utter silence, pumping, humming. I had left my fur with Wes so the shooter could see I was unarmed, and I was colder than I'd ever been in my life.

I reached the back of the store where the eggs and butter and milk and cheese waited on cold shelves to be taken away. I kept my eyes away from them and focused on the swinging doors leading to the storage area at the back of the store.

—I'm Assistant District Attorney Denise Lemoyne, I heard myself call out. My voice sounded cool and measured, but it was coming from some Observer within, at a great distance from me.

No sound came from the storage area. I realized my fists were clenched so tightly my nails were cutting into the palms of my hands. Then I heard something like a sob come from behind the swinging doors.

—I'm coming in, I said, and pushed my way through them.

The storeroom was enormous and dark. Piles of boxes and crates reaching far above my head were stretched out in long rows and vanished in the shadows. Some hand trucks lay stacked nearby, and the floor directly in front of me was awash in opened cardboard boxes, cans and packages scattered about. Chef Boyardee, Campbell's Chunky Soup. Only a few light bulbs hung from the ceiling here and there. The fluorescent fixtures were turned off.

—I'm here. If you want to talk, let's talk, I said to the silence.

Nothing but silence. I closed my eyes, trying to adapt them to the darkness, straining to hear that sob again, anything to suggest the shooter was in the building. Still nothing. I wondered if he'd managed somehow to break out of the police perimeter that had been set up around the supermarket. There was a phone on the wall just behind me near the doors I had come through. It began to ring. I jumped nervously and reached for it.

—Let it go, baby, someone said from very close to me.

Then I felt something even colder than the room pressing against my neck.

—That's just your pals outside. They want to make sure the party's not too tough. Let 'em wonder. You from the D.A.'s office?

I bit my lip and nodded. Then I felt a hard push, and stumbled across the floor into the sharp edge of one of the opened packing boxes. I caught myself, turned, and saw him for the first time.

He was enormous: a white man well over six feet with broad shoulders, a thick chest, and deep-set dark eyes that seemed to burn out of the shadows at me. He was wearing a cheap windbreaker, either black or dark blue, and a bright stream of glistening blood ran down his right shoulder. He was breathing hard as if he'd been running for blocks.

—Okay. So we make a deal, and you walk me out of here. Then I give you the slope.

Only then did he pull the young girl out from behind a big cardboard box. She sprawled at his feet with a small cry.

She was Vietnamese, probably seventeen, but she looked much younger. Her hair was in disarray, and her lips were quivering. Her eyes, dark and luminous, were fixed on the man's face. A wave of anger at her plight swept away my own fear.

—Let her up, I almost shouted at him. —Let her stand on her feet.

—Forget it. We do a deal, then we talk about her. Right now, she don't even exist.

—If you hurt her, they'll kill you, I told him in as matter-of-fact a voice as I could manage.

—Who will? The gooks? Shit, I killed more gooks than they got in this town.

—No. Captain Ralph Trapp of homicide. He doesn't like hostage-takers. And he especially doesn't like creeps who play meat games with women. If you hurt either one of us, he'll see you never make Central Lockup.

His eyes opened wide. I'd scored.

—Trapp? Not that black bastard again.

—You know him?

—Shit, everybody knows him. He fucked me up be-fore. Messed up my mouth. I had to get dental surgery

Good, I thought to myself. That could walk us. The girl hadn't moved, but she was staring up at me as if I had her destiny in my hands. Maybe I do, I thought.

—Here's the deal, I started.

—What?

—You let the girl go now. Then I walk you out to a police car and ride with you down to Central Lockup.

—What the fuck kind of deal is that?

—That's the one where you get out of here alive.

—No, look. I'm gonna give you the name of the man who bought the hit for that broad on the parking roof ... like who paid me. You get him, and I cop a plea to discharging a firearm or some ...

—What have you been toking back here? I heard myself say in a tone of astonishment. It must be Wes's and Rat's conversational style rubbing off on me.

—I got to have a deal. . . .

—I don't plea-bargain in a warehouse with a man holding a hostage. We'll talk about what you know at Central Lockup.

—Lady, you're trying to fuck me over. Maybe I ought to take you out for openers.

He began screwing a piece of blued metal tubing onto the muzzle of a long-barreled pistol. I felt panic rising and I edged away from the crates and toward the double doors as the phone began ringing again. On impulse I knocked the phone off the hook and let it fall dangling. I could hear a small distant voice calling my name. I couldn't recognize the voice on the other end, but I knew who it had to be.

—If you pull the trigger now, I said loudly, only the least tremor in my voice, —they'll hear it. Won't you, Rat . . . ?

The small metallic voice was yelling at me through the phone as it turned on its twisted cord. The big man had fallen silent. The girl seemed to have removed her-self from what was going on. Her dark eyes now roved about the gloomy stretches of the storeroom. I tried to follow what she was looking at. I heard a fly buzzing somewhere between us.

—You want the guy who bought the hit? the big man finally said, his voice softer, less assured.

—Sure I want him. And we'll deal on him. Later.

—You ride downtown in the same car with me?

—Right.

—No bullshit.

—No. You have my word.

He stepped out from the shadows and set the gun down on a case of Tampax. He nudged the girl to her feet. She stood up, but made no attempt to run, even to move.

—Do you understand English? I asked her.

She nodded.

—Then go. Walk slowly through the store, out to the front door. Wait until they see you, who you are. They'll call you to come out.

She stared at me for a moment, then moved through the swinging doors that led into the store so fast that I could hardly follow her with my eyes.

I picked up the silenced pistol and held it down by my side. Somehow it seemed absurd that I'd be walk-ing this hulk outside. He towered over me by at least a foot. He wasn't looking at me then, but toward the doors that still moved back and forth gently from the girl's passage.

—All right, I said, —let's move.

—Side by side, he said. —Not me in front. That crazy nigger might . . .

As we moved out into the bright light of the store, it seemed somehow things had returned to normal. The labels on cans and boxes had receded to their ordinary anonymity—of no significance unless they marked the brand you wanted to buy. But the whole place seemed to have a peculiar glow. As if I had been removed from the ordinary for a little while and suddenly returned to it.

Halfway down the aisle, I paused. —Have you got another gun? I asked the big man.

He grinned even though the blood from his shoulder had started pulsing out again.

—You want to strip-search me, baby?

—Keep moving, I said, thinking, what do I know about making an arrest? I'm only supposed to put them away. I'm not supposed to catch them.

At the door, Wes and Rat came up to meet us. Rat grunted with approval as he took control of the hulk. Wes, his face unusually pale, pulled me into a bear hug. I'm sure I was grinning like an idiot because I had somehow pulled it off. Then I remembered it wasn't quite over yet.

I turned my attention to Rat. His eyes widened as he looked into the big man's face.

—Well, shit. It's Malaporte. . . . Which one?

Malaporte watched him cautiously, hands in the air.

—Santorini.

—How you been, Santo old buddy? Rat smiled, giving him a short hard deadly accurate nudge with the heel of his hand right ovr the shoulder wound. Malaporte went pale, his knees going soft under him. He landed on the hood of the nearest patrol car, and Rat turned him face down.

—Rat. . . I said, as he cuffed Malaporte hard and tight.

—Yeah, honey. You okay?

—I'm riding downtown with him.

—Huh?

—That's the deal.

—What kind of deal?

—He wants to get there alive.

Rat looked pained. He lifted Malaporte from the car hood by his hair.

—Santo baby, when did I ever give you that bad notion?

—Come on, honey, Wes said to me. —The heroics are over.

—A deal's a deal, I said.

Rat handed Malaporte over to some uniformed patrolmen, than stared at me.

—Vote of no confidence, huh?

—No. He wanted to cop a plea back there. I can't deal that way on my own. But I had to give him something.

—Something is, you ride downtown to keep me off him?

—That's what he bought.

—Goddamn shame. I was gonna give him a kidney transplant on the way over to the lockup. Swap his left and his right. I'd of had your case in my pocket when we got there.

—Captain . . .

He shrugged.

—Come on, Counselor, he said in a disgusted tone, taking in Wes with his glance. —Let's all go together. You check me, I watch Santo, and Wes can keep his eye on all of us.

CHAPTER
2

B y the time we reached Central Lockup, newspeople and TV crews were already there, and one or two of the reporters called to us, but Wes kept his arm around me until we were inside. I still had the silenced pistol in my hand, and passed it over to one of the uniformed officers we met, telling him to log it into the property room as evidence in the Santorini Malaporte case.

—That's gonna look sweet on the six o'clock news, Wes grinned. —Pistol-packing prosecutor.

—But that's not my...

—How do they know? My story's gonna read, "She walked into the supermarket. She was colder than the air-conditioning. Malaporte never heard her coming. He didn't realize there was a .38 special in a charming petite lady's model with the stylish half-chromed two-and-a-half-inch barrel aimed at the back of his skull until she whispered suggestively, 'Okay, wop. Lose your iron, or I'll make Kitty Litter out of your face.'"

That did it. I began laughing until tears came, and I had to lean against Wes to keep from falling down. I'd done it somehow, and now that it was behind me it all seemed so absurd I couldn't stop laughing as Rat and two officers led Malaporte back to a holding cell.

Wes got me a cup of coffee, and we sat down in Rat's office. I was doing better then, except every so often, I'd start laughing uncontrollably again.

—Kitty Litter, I gasped.

—I've got to write that novel, Wes was saying. —Why should material like that go to waste in a lousy newspaper?

—You really wanted to stop me, didn't you?

Wes pulled me to him and kissed me.

—I would have, too, he said. —Except Rat had hold of my arm. I'd have had to leave the arm with him if I ran after you.

—Maybe next time I won't have to do it, I said, taking a deep breath.

Just then, a plainclothes detective passed by the open office door, the Vietnamese girl with him. She saw me, paused, smiled, and bowed ever so slightly.

—She's why I had to, I told Wes.

—Yeah, well, if you're into the duty thing, there's always a reason. But next time you think about playing Police Woman, remember I love you. I couldn't handle writing your obit.

He kissed me again and this time with feeling. Even with people sitting around, I couldn't help kissing him back.

Wes had just finished phoning in his story to the *Item* when Rat joined us. He sat down behind his desk and stared at me for a long moment. I tried to set myself for whatever kind of criticism he might level at me

—You did real good, he said at last. —You shouldn't have done it. You didn't have to do it. But you did fine.

—Thank you, I said. —Now what?

—Maitland called. The D.A. thinks you're . . . simply super.

—His words?

—Bet your sweet butt. You ever hear me talk that way? He wants you to prosecute the case.

—Oh God . . . the publicity, right?

—Listen, Dora-Bell, this here is show biz. You know Maitland.

Yes, I knew him. He'd been an assistant district attorney under my father's administration. John Maitland was an indifferent lawyer and a wretched person. No one had a good word to say for him professionally— but he came from an old New Orleans family with impeccable credentials, had the mandatory law degree from Tulane, and had managed to collect enough political debts over the years to put together just the right kind of coalition at election time. Now the D.A.'s office was going to be the greatest show in southeast Louisiana if Maitland could bring it off.

I tried to keep my mind on my own affairs. There was nothing I could do about Maitland and office policy. But I could do my job well.

—I want to talk to Malaporte. If it's my case, I can deal with him, find out why . . .

Rat smiled. A soft engaging sly smile. I knew he'd been up to something.

—Well, Counselor, lemme fill you in a little on that.

I knew what was coming, so I sat back with what was left of my coffee and listened as Rat played one of his favorite games: briefing me on the lowlife of New Orleans.

—Seems Santo-baby got himself a five-bill contract to

kill that pretty little blond deputy . . . from her husband. Used-car dealer named Lazy Louie Donovan. Lives in a fake Southern mansion out in Jefferson Parish.

—Santo must be down on his luck, Wes said.

—You know him? I asked.

—Sure. Didn't you recognize him?

—He seems familiar, but I can't remember where I've seen him.

—Bodyguard for the late Franco Xavier Burnucci.

That was it. He had a twin brother—Rat had called them "the bookends." He and his brother had been like a double shadow around the old man who'd run vice in New Orleans for years. I had seen them outside Burnucci's suite when he had gone into Sacre Coeur Hospital a couple of months before for some court-supervised tests. He had come out dead.

—A professional killer? But why was he doing an odd job for a used-car dealer?

—The old order changeth, Rat explained. —One day you're looking out for Franco Burnucci, dropping folks in the river when he frowns. Next day, you can't find a job with Orkin. When old man Burnucci was gathered to his daddies, his nephew, Kenny Amadeo, took over the family. Word is, the new *capo* decided to clean house.

Wes nodded and translated this for me. —In the old days, every time there was a little disagreement between gentlemen of eminence, the streets filled up with bodies. Santo was useful then. He could fill you a street, two alleys, and seven driveways with stiffs before you could say *basta*.

—But now Santo-baby's just an embarrassment, Rat put in. —Kenny's New Wave. Kenny don't need that. Nobody needs that.

—What about Donovan? I asked Rat.

—Lazy Louie is in the grasp, Rat said. —I had a squad car pick him up out at his used-car lot, sitting next to the phone sweating like a turkey in November.

—Santo used to do things right, Wes was saying. —What went wrong?

—Well, seems Malaporte stalked Janna Donovan, followed her in from Jefferson Parish, and took a shot at her as she got out of her car at the supermarket. But she leaned down to pick up her purse just as he pulled the trigger. He was silenced, but the shot blew her windshield all to hell. That, as you would say, put the wind up the little lady.

—Ha, Wes said.

—Did Donovan tell Malaporte his wife was a police officer? I asked.

—No...no, he didn't, Rat drawled. —Santo says he figures Donovan didn't want to pay extra. Cops are a premium hit.

—Donovan was trying...to save money?

—So it seems. Santo swears he wouldn't even break a cop's legs for less than ten grand. Not even a copperson's. He thought he was going for an easy five, but if it can go wrong, it's likely to, huh?

We sat quiet then. Rat chuckled and brushed his hand over his face. Wes simply shook his head. The two of them thought it was funny. I understood, even if most of the humor was lost on me. They had seen so much death over the years that an attempted murder, a kidnapping, and a hostage situation that had come out well was a positive relief.

—Santo Malaporte staring at twenty to life is worth at least a bottle of champagne, Rat said. —Lunch is on me.

—First I want to get Malaporte's statement in writing, I said.

—Haw, Rat answered. —You'll get heat prostration trying. Santo's gonna have lockjaw when you show.

—But he already told you . . .

—Private conversation. No steno.

—You read him his rights?

—Yes indeed. You know me. By the book.

I stared upward, but no relief was in sight. If you hear Rat Trapp is going by the book, you'd better check the title.

—See, Rat went on, —Santo just wanted to make sure we got Lazy Louie before he heard how things went down and cut out for Mexico or Tibet. Santo wants Louie lame and locked.

—So he can deal for immunity.

—You know it. Louie's all salted down and shelved. But you got to have Santo's statement to arraign and indict, which means you got to cut him a deal he likes. Face it, Counselor. You can have one from column A or one from column B, but not both at the same time.

—Shit, I said.

—Denise . . . Wes said, putting on his mock-shock look.

—I'm going to see Maitland, I said, as I got up and headed for the door.

The meeting with District Attorney Maitland was a waste of time. I could have written the script—and my own orders—without even bothering to go to his office. When it was done, I was ready for something stronger than the champagne Rat had offered.

When we reached Galatoire's, Rat was already sitting at his usual table back near the waiters' station. He rose as we joined him, and I noticed women in the restaurant throwing him admiring glances. Ralph Trapp refuses to look like a cop. If I had to guess, I'd say he was a special assistant to the mayor. He'd just changed to his winter wardrobe a few weeks before, and it would be deep in the season before he got all the way through it. Rat's not a dandy. He dresses well because he's found it useful.

Before I'd gotten situated, a dry martini with one small spiced olive was sitting in front of me. Rat leaned toward me with a grin and gestured toward Wes.

—Why don't you tell your boy there to go away? I'm sure that Mercedes of yours needs washing, honey.

Wes frowned, pretending to be confused as he sat down. —I didn't know he liked women, he said to me.

Rat turned and stared at him. —Even if I liked boys, you wouldn't cut it. Now if I had a mind for sheep . . .

—Okay, sheepfucker, what's on the menu today? Wes asked.

I tried to cut in as I saw Rat's smile growing. But it was too late, and there went any appetite at all for my favorite entrée.

—May I suggest the . . . rack of lamb?

—Oh, God, you bastards. You know how I love it here, I protested.

—You rack it? Wes asked Rat.

—Set the screws myself. Screamed and screamed, smiled and smiled. Sheepishly.

—How could you? I asked them.

—It was easy, they said in unison.

After the appetizers, things calmed down. I mentioned to Rat that Maitland had told me to go after Donovan. I had authority to plea-bargain Santorini Malaporte. He dropped his fork into his rémoulade and shook his head.

—That's the wrong choice, Dennie.

—Would you rather the principal walked?

—Lazy Louie? Hell yes. Louie ain't bad. He just wanted the community property and the insurance on his old lady. He sees he was wrong. He'll settle for a divorce now.

—He'll take ten to twenty for conspiracy to commit murder.

—I'd rather put the time on Santo. He fucks folks up.

—We can't always have what we want.

Wes and Rat exchanged a glum look. —Yeah, Wes said, —and life is very long.

—Not with Santo milling around it's not, Rat put in. —First nutbag wants to ground you and shows five grand...

—This is what the D.A. wants. I don't make the rules... or the judgment calls, either. So why are you giving me a bad time?

—I'd give it to District Attorney Maitland, baby, but he don't associate with ordinary cops.

—Damn it, Rat, I told him. —You know the system as well as I do.

—Yeah, we all know the system, Wes put in. —They ought to make a video game out of it. On the cover, you could have a picture of Justice blindfolded and grinning. With Santo Malaporte's hand up her dress. Call it Crazy Lady.

Rat shrugged and reached for his fork to scoop up some rémoulade. —As for my man Santorini, I guess we'll have to handle him on the street.

—Don't say that in front of me, I told him.

—You gonna give him police protection, Denise? Shit, let it be me.

I thought Maitland was making a mistake. Maybe we should be plea-bargaining Donovan to testify against Malaporte. But the rules I never made said that that afternoon I'd have to offer Malaporte a reduced charge

to get his testimony against Lazy Louie Donovan. I
didn't like it, but then nobody cared whether I liked it.

When I hit the office after lunch, there was a note that
they'd have Malaporte processed and in a holding cell
over at Central Lockup in an hour. I had plenty of
paperwork to keep me busy, and Santo wasn't going
anywhere. One of the first things you learn in the prac-
tice of law is that nothing happens with dispatch.
Things either grind on for months, or they happen in
seconds. I could smell grind in this Donovan mess.

Finally, an hour later, I walked across to Central
Lockup and checked in. When I reached the rank of
holding cells, I saw someone down at the end standing
in front of a cell, talking and gesturing. I thought I recognized him. I should have. It was Wes. He was talking
to Santo Malaporte.

—What are you doing in here? I asked him.

He turned, looking embarrassed. Almost. —What do
you say, sweetheart?

—I thought you were doing desk work this afternoon?

—Well, every so often, I like to take a break, and . . .

—. . . drop by and talk to the animals.

—You got it.

He glanced into the cell. —Hang in there, Santo, the
system's on your side. You got a bail hearing in the
morning.

Wes looked back at me, that faint wry smile in place.
I wasn't used to being its target. Normally I could share
Wes's humorous view of life, but somehow I sensed
this time the joke was on me.

—Piece of cake, he continued to Malaporte. —The
system says you put up chump-change, and you walk.

From inside the cell, I heard a coarse laugh.

—I'll pick you up after work, Wes said, turning to me. Then he winked and left before I could call him back.

Malaporte was harder to deal than I'd anticipated. His eagerness in the supermarket storeroom had turned to caution. He told me he had nothing to say until he was represented by counsel. He'd be needing a Legal Aid attorney for the bail hearing. After that, he'd manage for himself.

I worked on other cases until Wes showed up about five-thirty with the late edition of the *Item* in hand. His story on the supermarket shooting had made the front page—but barely. Two columns in the lower-left corner. Our little local violence was sloughed over by another terrorist attack in Italy in which seventeen had died.

Wes took me in his arms. —Sure it's small. They only run with the ones where people die. We don't want a big story. Not about us. Maybe just a small, discreet wedding announcement. After the fact.

We drove Uptown to his apartment. Wes made drinks and took out one of his favorite twenty-four-ounce steaks to put on the broiler.

—I can't eat any of that. I'm almost two pounds overweight now, I told him.

He smiled and kissed me. —You've had a big day, Dennie. You need protein.

But he put the steak aside and joined me on the sofa.

I shook my head as I remembered how I had felt inside the supermarket. —It was like . . .

Wes nodded. —Like a drug trip, all of your senses heightened. The ordinary world fell away and . . .

I laughed. —Oh, God, you're writing in your head again.

—It's true, isn't it?

I thought about it for a while. —I guess it is. How did you know?

—I've been there a couple of times. I may be there again, but I'm sure as hell not volunteering. I don't want you to, either.

The cynical smile was gone. He put his hands on my hips and drew me close to him.

—I want us to live a long time, sweetheart. I want us to grow old and cross and gray-headed together. I want the kids to come on Sundays and the grandchildren to wreck the sofa and spill ice cream on your best rug.

—I didn't know you had things planned that far ahead.

—I started planning the first time I looked out that library window at your house, and there you were.

We kissed again and began undressing. I wondered casually if Wes realized that every time he talks like that, I begin to get excited. As if it's already time to start on that family. Even before the wedding.

Our bodies knew each other well by then, but we hadn't begun to exhaust the mysteries we discovered each time we made love. That evening Wes cherished me more than before. He massaged my neck and back, relaxing and arousing me at the same time.

Then he looked down at me, and his expression was more serious than I had ever seen it.

—I can't make you not walk into the guns, he whispered. —All I can do is ask.

—Sometimes, I began, then had to start again as his hands made me shiver. —I have duties, just like you, I said softly, duty the last thing on my mind.

—I'm not going to let mine kill me, he said harshly, lovingly. —Not if I can help it.

—Me either, I whispered. —I promise, darling.

—When we're married, Wes said slyly, —what do you say I do the supermarket shopping?

We laughed and kissed again, and then the long day and everything that had happened fell away and the world itself narrowed to the warm musty confines of that bedroom as we made love and celebration for what seemed a long, long time.

It was much later when I noticed that the north wind blowing in the open door to the courtyard had chilled our sweat-drenched bodies. I rose and started dressing as Wes roused himself.

—Honey, how come you always leave? Why not spend the night with me? Hell, why not just move in?

I paused before I answered, not sure myself. I loved Wes, and the same thought had crossed my mind dozens of times when I found myself alone in the house on State Street. I think my reticence had something to do with an unexpressed fear—that Wes was an alien in New Orleans, only visiting for so long as it amused him or served his career. And that when he got ready to go he'd pack his bags in an hour and leave, not even looking back.

I wasn't sure I could put my life in a suitcase and move on, or even that I wanted to. New Orleans had always been my family's home. I'm sure I'd never thought of leaving. But the deeper my commitment to Wes became, the more certain it seemed my whole life would be changed, changed utterly.

And if I stayed in New Orleans, with Wes or... otherwise, there were certain standards that were quietly insisted upon. The rest of the country was free to do what it wished in the way of blatantly ignoring old standards of conduct. But not Uptown. Not just yet.

—I have to go home, I said, telling only half a truth

—My clothes . . . everything's there. I have court tomorrow morning.

I drove out to State Street, to the big empty house I still called home because I couldn't bear to sell it, move away from a place where I'd been so happy—and so lonely. I took a long hot bath, then sat in front of my mother's old vanity mirror brushing my hair with her silver-mounted brush, wondering if it made any sense for me to go on doing what I was doing.

It had been a long day. It wasn't the time to plan great changes in my life. I climbed into a cold empty bed, pulled a satin comforter over my head, and missed the warmth I had left at Wes's place.

Next morning, when I arrived in Division "I" of Orleans Parish Criminal District Court, Judge Elena Quintero's courtroom, Santorini Malaporte was already there, dressed as if he were on his way to a business meeting in Las Vegas. His arm was in a sling, but it didn't seem to bother him.

As I watched him during the other hearings, I realized that Malaporte was good-looking in an obvious, cheap way. His face had that dark bluish sheen of a man who never seems clean-shaven. When his own hearing began, he kept his hands in his lap and his head down as he listened to Rat Trapp answering my questions.

—So you know Santorini Malaporte, Captain?

—We've . . . bumped into one another.

—In what connection?

—He was a bodyguard and button man for Franco Burnucci.

—Button man?

—Burnucci would tell him to go kill somebody. Santo went and killed them.

—Objection, Malaporte's court-appointed defense almost shouted. —No foundation for such an accusation.

—Sustained.

—Do you, of your personal knowledge, know of any acts of violence perpetrated by the defendant?

—Yeah. He tried me on a couple of times over at Sacre Coeur Hospital a while back. When Burnucci was in there doing his dying.

—What exactly did he do?

—Pulled a gun on me.

—And . . . ?

—I took it away from him, hit him up side the head with it, emptied the chamber and the clip, and threw it at him.

—Was this in the line of duty?

—Uh, yeah. It was business . . . but I thought of it as pleasure.

—Objection . . .

It went on like that for ten minutes. Every time Rat would say something outrageous, the Legal Aid man would object, Elena Quintero would sustain and frown at Rat. He'd flash her a big smile, and she'd look away to keep from smiling back.

Finally, she called me and the Legal Aid man to the bench.

—I'm satisfied, Miss Lemoyne.

—Satisfied as to what, Your Honor? Legal Aid wanted to know. He had a nasty rattish face and a New York accent. He bit his fingernails.

—I'm satisfied Malaporte would shoot his mother if the bucks were right, Mr. Louper. I'm going to set bond at one hundred and fifty thousand dollars.

—On the word of one police officer? Your Honor . . .

—You've got that wrong, Judge Quintero said.

—Captain Trapp is at least three cops. Anyhow, I've read Mrs. Donovan's deposition. One-fifty, or he rots till he talks. You dealing with him, Denise?

I tried to look away, but Elena Quintero had a long glance. I nodded. She shook her head.

—I wish you didn't have to do that. I really do.

—Your Honor . . . Legal Aid started.

—Louper, you've come to a new town and a new job. Do you want to get along, or do you want your fanny boiled in a forty-gallon drum every time you have a motion in front of me? It's all up to you.

I managed to keep a straight face till I got back to the prosecution table. The judge was still filling Mr. Louper in on how to survive and flourish in Orleans Parish Criminal District Court. I liked Elena Quintero a lot. She was the down side of forty, but her skin didn't tell a thing. She had dark straight hair pulled back and rolled at the base of her skull, and enormous brown eyes that could freeze or melt, depending on her intention. I hoped at forty I'd have a figure like hers. She wore whatever she liked, and it all looked wonderful on her. At an outdoor barbecue last Labor Day, I recalled she'd worn her hair straight down her back, a peasant blouse, a flowing skirt clasped around her small waist, and ballerina slippers. She had every male head turning, then turning again.

Finally she sent Legal Aid packing back to his seat, assigned the bail, and called a recess for lunch. I glanced over at the defense table. Malaporte was patting Legal Aid on the back as if he'd done something wonderful. Then I saw him look toward the rear of the courtroom. Benny Temenos was scuttling up to the clerk's desk with an attaché case he must have found at the city dump. Benny writes bonds. If he can get the right collateral, he'll bail Jack the Ripper. Does Attila the Hun have any immovable property? What kind of pledges could Hitler or Stalin come up with?

Why was Benny shaking hands with Santo Malaporte? I wondered. The bond was one-fifty. From what Rat had told me I doubted Santo could make ten thousand, and Benny, one of the aristocracy of bondsmen, doesn't write for losers—or for people he'll have to go find.

Rat was standing outside the bar just behind me.

—Ah . . . he sighed, his eyes pointed the same way as mine. —What do you think, Counselor?

—Maybe Kenny Amadeo's strong on family feeling and decided he owes Santo.

Rat laughed. —You may be right. Santo does know a lot of stuff. Old family retainer stuff. They don't hang dirty linen out to dry.

—They could bail him and bump him, I said.

—Yeah, they could. That's a great idea, Dennie.

—Rat . . .

Sure enough. Benny pulled some papers from the shambles of his briefcase, handed them to Malaporte who signed them. Then Benny passed them to the clerk. Malaporte gave me a wink and a nod on his way out.

—That was a nice name for the system Wes came up with.

—Huh?

—Crazy Lady, Rat said in disgust, and followed Malaporte and Benny out of the courtroom.

As I was fitting my file folders into my attaché case, Madeline St. Juste came up to the bar.

—Hi, I said. —Were you here for the whole show?

She was dressed in a rust-colored gabardine suit that seemed to touch her freshly set blond hair with a hint of auburn. I'd never seen her look lovelier or younger. It was hard to believe she was the same woman I'd seen at St. Louis Cemetery the day before. She shook her head at my question.

—Just the last case. I'd read about it in the *Item*. That man shouldn't be out on the street.

—No, I said wearily. —No, he shouldn't. But . . .

Madeline had half-turned, her eyes fixed on the doors of the courtroom where Malaporte had passed through moments before.

—I wonder if René knows him? she asked, more nearly a question to herself than to me.

—René? My God, I hardly think so. Paid killers don't run with our kind of people.

—I suppose not, she mused. —Still . . .

—Whatever put that in your mind?

Madeline wasn't looking at me. She still had her eyes fastened on those closed wooden doors. As if she expected Santorini Malaporte to walk back through them again. Her gaze was so intense that I found my own eyes following hers, so I wasn't looking at her when she spoke again.

—Sometimes I think . . .

—What?

—I think René might hire someone like him. To have me killed.

CHAPTER

3

We were in the warm brick-walled atmosphere of the Pontchartrain Hotel's Caribbean Room, poised over martinis by the time I got my breath. Madeline was laughing.

—Darling, forget it. It was just a silly thing that popped into my mind. What do they call it? Word association? You must have learned about it in psychology classes.

—Not funny, Madeline. If Janna Donovan hadn't been highly trained and very lucky...

Madeline cut me off with a nervous gesture of her hand. Her expression wasn't cheerful anymore.

—It must have been a terrifying experience for her. Someone in the courtroom said her husband just couldn't find a way . . . to ask for a divorce.

—That's one I hadn't heard, I said. —More likely Donovan couldn't stand the idea of parting with half the community property.

Madeline shrugged and toyed with a platinum cigarette lighter she'd taken from her purse.

—I know it sounds absurd, but I believe it happens.

—What? I really don't see . . .

—I think . . . people married for a long while can
grow apart . . . intimately.

—Sorry?

She turned the lighter one way, then the other. I
couldn't help noticing that her hands had been marked
by the years: they were unblemished but the veins now
stood out prominently and the long manicured nails
made her fingers almost clawlike. Finally she lit her cigarette, the tiny flame from her lighter reflected in the
old-fashioned gold-and-diamond scallop-shell earrings
she wore. A matching brooch, probably a piece from
her mother's estate, gleamed discreetly at the neck of
her silk blouse.

—Things build up between married people. Things
they don't want to say, can't bear to . . . talk about. It
would be easier for one of them to . . . kill the other than
to mention certain things.

—Oh, Madeline, that sounds . . .

—Ummm. You haven't been there, dearest. You
haven't visited the cavern they call marriage yet. It's
very deep and dark. The silences can grow and grow
. . . until they scream at you. Until . . . all you can hear is
what . . . neither of you ever says.

—I really *don't* understand . . .

Madeline lifted her drink, drained it, and gestured to
our waiter.

—You know, of course, that René is almost six years
younger than I, she said almost formally.

While I'd never known his exact age, René St. Juste
had always seemed younger, at least in spirit, than

Madeline. I'd always liked her husband. He was warm and friendly, handsome and pleasant in the British tweeds he affected when he was at home or driving over to the Holman country place near Mandeville, across Lake Pontchartrain.

René had taught me how to ride, and had played the part of the older male admirer that every young woman dreams of. Nothing romantic, certainly nothing sexual —at least not in the contemporary style. Simply a certain way his eyes touched me, moved over me, his hands catching my reins, guiding me, pressing me to do my best.

My image of him the summer of my sixteenth year, in tweeds and leather astride his stallion, racing along a misty Mississippi levee, would have easily served as cover art for a romantic novel. I smiled at the remembrance, then saw from Madeline's drawn expression that she was waiting for some response.

—Oh, really? I said lamely.

—Oh yes, very really. Then her second martini arrived, and she took quick refuge in it before going on. —And, as fate or God or statistics or some other nasty thing would have it, we've never had any children.

—Oh, I blurted out before I thought, —you wanted them? I always supposed the two of you chose not to . . .

Madeline's small laugh sounded like broken crystal falling from her lips. I could see that there were tears in her green eyes.

—The carefree wealthy Uptown couple, too much in love, having too much fun to let a little René or a little Madeline interfere with the grand design?

—I didn't intend it that way.

—Of course you did. But the fact is . . . we tried for

years. A number of specialists said René's to blame. Of course, he won't accept that. He blames me.

She fell silent, her eyes on the tablecloth. I could see that she was biting her lip.

—I don't see anyone's to blame for a medical problem, Madeline.

She laughed out loud at that. Heads turned at other tables. Madeline waved for our waiter. Before she could ask for another martini I asked for menus. It looked as if Madeline might be on her way to drinking lunch. I couldn't bear for her to be embarrassed in public. It wasn't her image I wanted to protect. It was her.

—Oh, Denise darling, in life, in a marriage, you forgive each other nothing... nothing at all. I suppose one can't afford to. The struggle is usually too close, too harrowing. There are no truces. You never take prisoners. And you keep very careful books. One or the other of you is to blame for... everything.

—Has René said he blames you for not having children?

Madeline lit a cigarette, considered my words.

—I think... yes. He did. Once. It's moot now. I'm into menopause. It's simply not an issue any longer. But it carries over. It gets added in with the rest.

—The rest? What else is there?

—Ummm. There's money, of course.

—But René's always done well in oil. Hasn't he?

—With my father's contacts and some of my money, he's managed very well. Over twenty years of success. I imagine it becomes a habit, success. I couldn't say from personal experience.

—Then...

—Denise, don't you read the papers? Those idiots in OPEC have let the whole thing fall apart. Oil has gone to hell. Texas mansions are on the auction block. Half the independents in Louisiana are out of business, carrying the equipment and outfitting and service companies down with them. No one wants René's land leases. He couldn't give them away. In a few more months, he'll be ruined.

—I'm so sorry.

—Don't be. At least not on my account. I've decided I'm not staying for the last act. The silences between us have become too long. But René's demanding I help him.

—Help him?

—With Momma's money. She left me her estate. It's ... really quite something. And I won't throw it away on a business that's gone bad. For a man who...

Madeline's voice trailed off. I supposed her mother's estate truly must be something. Word had it that her family's land holdings near Baton Rouge and west had been immense. Heloise Boileau Holman's money had started her husband's career in New Orleans when he had come south from Shreveport in the early 1930s. Now Aunt Heloise's estate belonged to Madeline.

—That's why I simply had to talk to you. I want a divorce... but I want it to be discreet. Do you understand?

—Of course, but shouldn't you...?

—If you mention counseling or some other vulgarity, I'll get up and leave.

I was embarrassed. I *had* been about to suggest a priest or marriage counselor, but in bad faith. I didn't believe in such things, either. Women in our set hadn't quite managed to accept a world in which one discussed marital infidelity, petty or great brutality, orgasms, unsuccessful or otherwise, with sympathetic religious or psychiatric functionaries. Even as a girl, I'd always found Tennessee Williams's famous line grotesque: Uptown New Orleans ladies never trust to the kindness of strangers—or anyone else, for that matter. We find what we need within ourselves, or we do without.

—And for God's sake don't suggest we talk it through, Dennie. Really, René and I have forgotten each other's languages. Come to think of it, we never talked much. When we started out, we did screw a lot. It was very nice. As far as it went.

I must have blushed. Madeline and René had almost been surrogate parents after my mother's death. One never thinks of parents as having a sex life. They're icons, fleshless, passionless, always in control. But I called to mind barely remembered teenage fantasies about René and recalled that I had envied Madeline. Yes, I thought, it must have been very nice.

Madeline set down her drink as the waiter put hot appetizers of Shrimp Saki before us. She seemed to interpret my prolonged silence as disapproval.

—Sorry, darling. You see, my *monologue interieur* isn't terribly tasteful any more. Even the *exterieur* could use some sprucing up, couldn't it?

As she ate, I could see she was doing her best to control emotions that didn't want to be controlled. She set down her fork and stared at the last shrimp swimming in lemon and spices and butter for a long moment. She searched for a smile and finally came up with one.

—All right, I'll try talking to him. Just so that I can say "I told you so" and get on with ending it.

—If you find there's really nothing to say, I'll call someone for you. There are some fine attorneys who can handle things . . . smoothly.

Her smile seemed real then.

—Ah, smoothly. That's the way everything in life should go, isn't it? Ever so nasty and twisted and spiteful—but smoothly. What was Talleyrand's recipe for diplomacy? Oh yes . . . "Please, no enthusiasm."

We finished the shrimp and started on the entrée before Madeline began talking again.

—Tell me about your young man, Dennie. He's quite nice-looking. In a rough-hewn sort of way.

I laughed. —I think he's rougher than he looks. Uncle Henry can tell you about that.

She nodded. —He *did* tell me. It seems Mr. Colvin is . . . resourceful. It was very clever of him to find out the awful things our families kept buried for so long. I suppose we even owe him thanks for keeping it to himself.

Madeline paused in the midst of a bite, an amused frown on her face.

—Of course, I shouldn't think any of us needs to marry him to show our appreciation.

I laughed as if it were a wonderful joke. At least Madeline was sounding like her natural biting self. Perhaps everything she'd said before was no more than the product of a bad mood generated by those hormones that trap us and spin us around when we near fifty. As to her remark about Wes, I knew she was serious. She could no more approve of him than she approved of her father, Henry Holman. She loved Uncle Henry, but she thought of him as a crude, hard, homespun backwoodsman from north Louisiana who had, with the help of his native amorality, abundant shrewdness, and her mother's money, made his way in New Orleans society despite everything. I tried to make my reply as dry as her remark.

—Oh, but I *do* think so, Madeline. I didn't have any choice, really.

—I beg your pardon?

—That was the bargain, didn't you know? Either I promised to marry Wes . . . or he told all.

—Good God, Denise . . .

—Whenever he has his way with me, I just think of Uptown honor. It helps ever so much.

Madeline burst out laughing.

—You scamp. Your *monologue interieur* is tackier than mine.

Her smile softened after a moment. —He makes you very happy, doesn't he?

—Yes, I said, simply, honestly. —He makes me feel . . . the way I want to feel. About myself, about my life. I'm never lonely with him.

—That's how it began with René and me. Oh, God, Dennie, if you could remember him twenty-five years ago. Tall, suntanned, the beau ideal of every black-eyed Cajun girl in Lafourche and Evangeline and St. Bernard parishes. He did all those outlandish things you hear about. Wrestled alligators, caught garfish by the gills and brought them into the boat bare-handed. René could dance, play the guitar. He used to take me to outrageous little gin mills on dirt roads miles from any civilization at all and start fights with the worst, ugliest, meanest bayou men he could find.

—René? I've never heard him raise his voice.

—He didn't raise it then. He'd simply say something insulting in Cajun French to some man in a . . . what did he call them? In a blind tiger, a roadhouse. They'd go outside and hit and tear and slash one another. In absolute silence, no sound but their grunting and straining.

—Good God . . . Wes isn't that way.

Madeline stared across the room at no one. —Of course not. None of them is. My father still reads Vir-

gil. When he's not out with men from the krewe, hunting and fishing and gutting and skinning.

She turned her attention back to me, her eyes bright
with anger. —Damn it, Denny, they're all . . .

She paused and took a bite of her food, then began
again, softly. —It's not the best idea to marry outside
your set. Nothing assures us happiness, but we're better off if we settle for something . . . less than exciting.

I laughed. Not in derision, but in surprise. —Marry
. . . for security? I think that's part of what having a career, being my own person, spares me. I'd never marry
safely. I just couldn't.

Madeline gave me a brittle smile and pushed her
plate aside. —Well, I suppose I'm not the one to be
giving advice. I put my life into my marriage. Long before women even thought about careers. The only
women who worked when I was young were those
who had no choice.

She turned thoughtful then. —Actually, if I had
everything to do again . . . Her smile was wide, genu-
ine. —Why, I'd choose something I wanted to do very
much. Something that could belong to me. Something
. . . that wasn't community property.

We had coffee afterward and talked about less monu-
mental things. Then, as we walked toward the door to
the hotel foyer, Madeline turned and kissed me impul-
sively.

—I want to get to know Wes Colvin. I truly do. Promise me we'll get together soon . . .

—Of course, I told her. —I still need your advice.

Madeline gave me a strange, loving look.

—That's very sweet of you to say, she said softly, as if
she'd had no idea how much I cared for her.

We kissed, and I walked out to St. Charles Avenue,
thinking Madeline would be coming along, too. But as I

pushed open the door, she turned aside into the dark bar off the main lobby, giving me a jaunty wave as the glass came between us and cool November air touched my face.

As I waited for my car to be brought around, I thought of a sentence Madeline hadn't finished. "They're all . . ." I wondered what she had in mind. All hunters? All brutal? All at last . . . unloving?

A moment later, I found myself giving the valet a cold assessing stare as I tipped him and climbed into my car. His eyes had met mine, then passed over me as if he were deciding whether I'd be a really fine lay, or just passable. I felt myself shiver as I pulled away from the curb and started down the avenue, and I realized that, without the slightest reason, I was angry as hell at Wes.

I soon had something like a reason. Marj, my secretary, looked up from her desk and handed me a telephone slip without a word.

—Maitland? I asked her, hoping perhaps that my boss had reconsidered the Malaporte business.

Marj shook her head. —Nope, not the Good Hood. It's from B-B 3-E.

Don't ask me where she gets the raw material for her personifications. Maitland, the boss of all bosses in the D.A.'s office, is the Good Hood. Rat Trapp is Dee-Dee. Short for Down and Dirty. B-B 3-E is Wes. It stands for the Big Bopper of the Third Estate.

The note simply said that Wes would have to miss supper that evening. He was up to his ears in a very big story. That didn't sound like Wes. He worked hard, but he never let anyone notice. And he hardly ever misses our dates. I suppose I still had Madeline's unfinished line in mind, but I found myself dialing his number at the *Item*. I asked the newsroom receptionist for Wes, but there was a long wait. Then someone else came on the line. I realized it was Henry Holman, publisher of the *Item*, Madeline's father—and my godfather.

—Uncle Henry, is that you?

—Sure is, honey. You looking for that boy of yours?

—I must have dialed the wrong number.

—Nope. Girl at the desk just put you on through. Wes has got himself a heavy-duty story coming down. He's likely to be at it most of the night.

—What's going on, Uncle Henry?

—Uh, nothing earthshaking. Just a hell of an idea for a feature series.

—Damn...

—Something I can do for you, honey?

—No. I'm just being childish. We had a supper date.

—Well, I'm sorry about that. But youall are gonna have all the time in the world for long suppers full of champagne and starlight and music. Right?

—I hope so. But I may have to make him quit the paper first.

—You don't want to do that, sugar. The boy's a natural. You keep law and order, and let Wes tell all the folks about it.

—I don't think that's the way he sees reporting.

—Ha. You may be right. If there's anything...

—No, thanks. It was good to talk to you.

I finished my report on the Malaporte case, did some paperwork, and drove back out to State Street. Carole, my maid, met me at the door.

—Long day?

—No, not really. It's just that... they all seem that way

—There's a nice rarebit warm in the oven. Don't let it dry out.

—How did you know I'd be in this evening?

—Wes called earlier. Said he was tied up and wanted to be sure you got the message.

I frowned as Carole picked up her coat and left. Why would Wes go to such lengths to make sure I knew he was breaking our dinner date? That damned half-sentence of Madeline's came back and teetered on the edge of my consciousness once more.

I felt suddenly, utterly, alone. As if there were no one in the world who knew or cared how I'd spend the long autumn evening. I hadn't felt that way in months. And I couldn't grasp why the feeling had come over me just then. Was I seriously questioning Wes and me? Had Madeline's absurd old-fashioned Uptown attitude raised doubts I'd never felt on my own?

I tried to think about it, but the more I turned it over in my mind, the sillier it seemed. If Madeline's marriage was going wrong, it wasn't because René St. Juste hadn't been born into that tight little Uptown New Orleans world of ours. Marriages go wrong every day, everywhere, and it has nothing to do with such things.

Or does it? I tried to imagine Wes and me married a dozen years. But I couldn't. I could see us in love, in bed, sailing on Lake Pontchartrain, riding horses in Audubon Park. But not living there on State Street, not married with children enrolled at Newman School— who would go on to Tulane or Newcomb and find places in the banks or professions or businesses of our friends.

Because my friends, the people I'd grown up with, weren't his friends. And they weren't likely to be, were they? For some reason I remembered a story my grandfather had told me once. When he was a bright young attorney, he had been introduced to Huey Long just after his election as governor of Louisiana. Huey had offered my grandfather a job, but Grandfather, already aware of Huey's loathing of our kind of people, turned him down. Huey had laughed and told my grandfather to come see him ... if he ever decided to serve the living instead of the dead. I'd never forgotten the story. Somehow I couldn't. As if it had been a curse that that north Louisiana barbarian Huey Long had placed on my family. If that's what it had been, it had functioned very well indeed. I was the last of the Lemoynes who had not yet entered that lovely chill temple in St. Louis Cemetery.

I sighed and wished it were still light. It was going to be an awful evening, a long night. There'd been burglaries in the neighborhood over the past few months. Nothing violent so far, but enough to make a woman alone listen to every sound. And my old house was a chorus of sounds. The wind outside made the whole enormous wooden structure moan and shudder. The floors and the great stairway creaked, the dry wood no longer limber and flexible as it had been a century before.

Just then the knocker on the front door sounded hollowly, and I almost jumped out of my skin. I sat collecting myself until it sounded once more, then went and peeked out a foyer window to see who was calling.

I opened the door breathing hard with relief.

—Uncle Henry, it's you ...

—It is. You look like something scared you. None of them burglars been around, have they?

—No, no. I suppose I just can't get used to winter being here. I hate the cold and the wind and the dark, don't you?

—I guess. But it's gonna get worse before it gets hot.

ter. The TV says there's another cold front on the way. Just passed through Shreveport and Natchitoches. Cold as a polar bear's behind, sweetie.

He followed me in a shuffling gait into the library. Henry Holman was nearing eighty, and the aggressive young redneck who had climbed from backwoods reporter to publisher of the most important newspaper in the state was finally slowing down a little.

I made him a drink and stoked the library fire.

—This is a social visit, isn't it?

—Nothing else, he said, his heavy reddish face fixed in a perpetual smile. —We haven't seen much of one another since Heloise's funeral, have we?

—Not enough, I told him. —But I lunched with Madeline today.

He smiled a little wider. —That's good. I've got to check in on her, too. She's been kinda down in the dumps lately. Losing her momma, I expect.

—I'm sure that's it, I said, not sure at all after what Madeline had told me.

—I came by to take Wesley's place, honey. Come eat with me, Henry said. —I'm going down on Dryades Street and have me a steak at Charlie's. But I'd as soon not face it all by myself.

—Uncle Henry, you know Dr. Lanier wouldn't approve of all that cholesterol. Your blood pressure . . .

—Gets higher when busybodies try to tell me how to live. We're not going to get out of this world alive, so let's enjoy the time we have. What do you say?

—Ten minutes to change? I asked.

He glanced down at his watch and nodded. —I'll make the usual translation and look for you in half an hour.

I laughed and ran upstairs. As I changed from my conservative office clothes into fawn-colored suede pants topped with a matching raw-silk sweater, I wondered if I should bring up the conversation Madeline and I had had.

As I sat before my mother's old mirror and pulled a comb through my dark-blond hair and added a touch of makeup, I considered it. And ended it where I would have expected to end: I'd say nothing. If Madeline wanted her father to know about her marriage coming apart, she'd tell him. There was a great sense of pride in her, and I suspected that Henry was the last person in the world she'd want to know.

When I returned to the library, the fire was burning low, the room looking even warmer, more comfortable than it felt. Henry was bent over an album of old family pictures, leafing through it page by page.

—Lord, Lord, he said. —Don't these old pictures take you back?

He was looking at a group photo of Madeline and me and a number of other women attired in suits and hats and gloves. We were all former queens of the Carnival Krewe of Pandora, and the photo had been taken a year or so before at a luncheon the krewe gave every year at Carnival for those who had reigned over its court through the generations.

—Is there still going to be a Krewe of Pandora? I asked him. It seemed a reasonable enough question. After all, Wes and I had met as he and Rat Trapp were in the process of proving that the carnival club was the remnant of a conspiracy from fifty years before.

Henry gave me a sly smile. —Why, honey, what makes you ask? Pandora's a part of New Orleans's history.

—But, Uncle Henry...

—Baby, surely you've heard of fossils? They're just critters who turned to stone and kept right on going when everything around them gave way to time. Just 'cause the heart and brain and purpose of an institution freezes is no reason to let it go. You need to read up on the Austro-Hungarian empire.

We both laughed. Because it was funny and true.

—Anyhow, Henry said, —I'm thinking of proposing some new blood for the krewe.

—Oh?

—Yeah. I nominated René St. Juste when he and Madeline got married. Worked out all right, I guess.

He turned pages in the picture album, past photos of my father, my grandfather. He was turning the pages backward, moving into the past. He didn't look up at me as he spoke.

—I was thinking of nominating Wes Colvin.

I started to answer, but Henry cut me off.

—Time the boy stopped being an outsider.

—I don't think that's likely, do you?

—Oh, Dennie, I wouldn't say that. Look at me. I used to think I'd never get north Louisiana out of my blood, but time and circumstance . . .

He fell silent, closed the book, and looked up at me.

—Bob Pleasance is gonna be retiring this January. He reckons on going back to Memphis or wherever he came from. I'm gonna be looking for a new city editor.

—Wes . . . ?

—He's smart. Maybe a little too smart, but like I say, time and circumstance . . . Someone's got to take over the *Item* after I . . . retire. It sure won't be René St. Juste. And you're almost as dear to me as Madeline. Why not give your boy a shot at it?

—Do you think Wes'd be interested? He likes rooting out a story. I don't know if he could stand being tied to a desk.

—I guess maybe that depends on you, honey. If you

want him to join the krewe, take the job, he just might
—'cause he sure as hell is interested in you.

Henry looked me over in the way a young man
might. Most likely I blushed.

—Henry, you know Wes . . .

—I do indeed. First time I saw youall together, I
knew him well enough. Country boy like Wes gets his
mind set on a woman, he won't let go till it thunders.

—I can't make him do anything, I said.

—Henry laughed out loud. —Girl, you don't have to
play sweet-innocent with me. All you got to do is let
him know what you'd like him to do. Believe me, I
know. We can make Wes Colvin a New Orleans boy in
spite of himself.

After supper at Charlie's, where I had a salad and
watched Henry demolish an enormous T-bone, we
walked outside. It was chill, and rain was falling fast
and hard. That cold front was on the way. I stood huddled in the doorway of the restaurant as Henry turned
up his collar and walked down Dryades Street to get
the car. I noticed an early edition of the *Item* in a vend-
ing machine by the door. Across the front page, a
headline jumped out at me:

THE HIT PARADE
by
John Wesley Colvin

I dropped my dime in the machine and held the
paper up to the weak neon light. It was the first in a
series of articles on the life and times, the corruption of
public officials, the executions and maimings that had
kept former mob boss Franco Xavier Burnucci un-
touched by the law through a long and profitable criminal career.

Henry pulled up in the car, and I got in, feeling the cold rain on my legs. Now I knew what Wes was working on. I handed Henry the copy of the *Item*.

—I wonder where Wes is getting his information, I said out loud. Henry looked over at the paper, then at me, and smiled.

CHAPTER

4

W hen I awakened the next morning, I was as tired as when Henry Holman had seen me to my door, waited for me to lock it behind me, and driven off in the rain with, for all I knew, that enigmatic smile still wreathing his face.

I'd tried every old country kinfolk's trick in the book to find out where Wes was getting his information for "The Hit Parade" series in the *Item*. Henry had shrugged. He didn't know. He hadn't asked Wes. If Wes had started to tell him—which he wouldn't— Henry would have told him to shut up.

—You folks down at the D.A.'s can't put me in jail for what I don't know, he'd told me, simply beaming.

—Meaning you think Wes might end up doing time for contempt of court?

—Why honey, that's between youall. Me? I just publish the damned paper.

As he had turned to go, he paused. —Of course, if Wes *does* do time, and gets a look at the inside of the

New Orleans lockup, that'd likely end up another series on the shame of our penal system. Don't you reckon?

That caution was on my mind when I got to the office. Copies of the *Item* were on all the desks. Even the secretaries were reading Wes's piece. I had the feeling every one of them was watching me as I walked by— and not because of my new navy-blue suit or my smashing legs.

—It's worth a special grand jury, Maitland said, his usual intensity turned up forty-six degrees. —Christ, with that kind of information, we could scour this town. Whoever Colvin's talking to has the map.

—Map?

—Colvin's source can finger every hit in this town since 1963.

—That's the year I was born, I said.

—Is that relevant?

—I don't think so.

—Talk to him, Maitland said. —I don't want to subpoena him. I don't want to shove him around. He's a good reporter.

—John, it's a waste of time. Anyhow, I think you're presuming on a personal relationship.

—Of course I am. Look, Denise, this office uses all its resources. If I had the relationship with Colvin . . . Maitland's voice broke off as I laughed.

—You know what I mean, he said sullenly.

—I suppose I do.

—So talk to him.

I stood up and nodded. Not because I wanted to, but because I was more than ready to end the meeting.

—I will talk to him. Then I'll pass on to you, uncensored, what Wes tells me to tell you.

—Tell him to make it easy on all of us.

—Oh, no. Wes never makes anything easy on anyone. And believe me, no matter what happens, it won't be a bit easier on me.

—I wouldn't say that, he muttered. —I value loyalty. We all value loyalty around here.

Maitland tried to smile. Then it hit me for the first time. The reason I disliked him so much was that he reminded me of my father.

The rain was still falling when I drove to Wes's apartment. I knew he'd have his phone off the hook at that hour, and anyhow, I had no intention of relaying Maitland's message over the phone. On top of that, since Maitland was so insistent, I thought I'd take a little holiday on office time.

I used my key to let myself in. Wes had to be under that comforter and those three pillows, but I couldn't be sure by just looking. For just a moment, I wanted to undress and climb in under the covers with him. It would be a nice way to start the day all over again.

But it wouldn't be right. Because this was close to an official visit. He was going to be mad as hell at what I had to ask him.

So I poured hot water through a drip pot full of CDM coffee, sat down by the computer work desk near his courtyard doors to watch the rain falling into the evergreens outside, and waited for the coffee to brew.

I noticed that the coffee table in front of Wes's tattered sofa was covered with scribbled sheets of yellow legal paper. There seemed to be dates and diagrams, a jumble of names and places. An empty whiskey bottle and two glasses stood next to an ashtray filled with cigarette and cigar butts. It seemed he'd been working and drinking late into the night. For a moment I considered picking up the papers and going through them as he slept. The answers to the questions I had to ask him might be scattered there.

Then I shook my head. That wouldn't be a very healthy way of nurturing our relationship, would it? I turned away from the table and looked outside.

The rain had softened to a gentle haze. It was dripping off the roof, making guttural sounds in the rainspout. The humidity must have been very high, because the rain seemed to meet mist rising from the gardenias and camellias around the courtyard's outer walls. It was as if the day itself were vanishing, as if the familiar old city out there were no more than a dream I'd had once.

Then I felt his lips touching my cheek. He slid a mug of hot coffee and chicory over to me and sat down across the small table very slowly, very carefully, the way I remember my grandfather doing when he was quite old. His skin was still brown from his summer suntan, but underneath it his face looked gray and exhausted.

—You read my article.

—Yes, and so has everyone else on the D.A.'s staff.

—It's good stuff. Henry even said it was local history.

—Maitland wants your source, I said, setting my cup down.

Wes smiled. —People in hell want ice water.

—People in hell can't subpoena you and your refrigerator, I told him. —They can't ask a judge to dunk you for the life of the grand jury. And then do it over and over again.

His eyebrows rose and he stared at me. —That creep sent you here to . . .

—He asked me.

—And you said yes.

—Maitland thinks he could clean up the town with a witness who can swear to what you've got in that article.

—Maitland couldn't clean his ass with a half-ton roll of newsprint.

—Don't talk to me like that, Wes. I don't want to hear it.

—I'm not real wild about you coming to my place, using your key, waking me up, and leaning on me.

—You'd rather talk to Maitland?

—Maitland is trash. He's a two-bit Uptown Tulane type who can't decide between boys and girls. He gets his law from assistants who are smarter than he is, and his style from reruns of "Perry Mason."

—Good God, Wes, does it always come back to that?

—To what?

—How can you stay in a town where you loathe everyone so much?

He laughed and turned back to the glass door that looked out on the rain-slick courtyard.

—It's the weather. I love the weather.

His familiar tone of contempt cut through my defenses. For a moment I was again the lonely little girl whose mother had died too soon and whose father had been too busy with his career to see that she needed his love.

—I thought you . . . loved me.

Sensing something of my pain, he turned back quickly, confusion in his eyes.

—I do love you, Dennie . . . except when you're playing Uptown New Orleans games with me.

—I'm not playing. Do you think I'm enjoying this? It's my job. Maitland told me to ask you for sources. He thought it would be better if I . . .

—It's not better. He can drag me in, throw me in the slammer. I'll use the time to write a book. Same name as the articles. No, I'll call it "The New Orleans Hit Parade," and the last chapter will be all about the New Orleans Parish D.A.'s office, and the wonderful people who let Franco Burnucci jerk the town around for fifty years.

—And the epilogue will be about me?

He rose from his chair quickly, pulled me up out of mine.

—Honey, go back and tell Maitland you ran his number past me. Tell him I laughed, and then you and I hit the sack and made love like a couple of Greek divinities.

He tried to draw me over to the bed, but I pulled away from him. I had wanted him when I first arrived, but it didn't feel right anymore. I loved Wes, but his contempt for New Orleans, for what the city is, what it has always been, kept pushing us apart. I started for the door.

Just as I reached it, I turned. There was something else I was supposed to tell him.

—Henry Holman wants to put you up for the Krewe of Pandora.

—Ha . . .

—He says Pleasance is retiring early next year. He'll need a new city editor, and . . .

—Jesus Christ, Wes said, looking at me as if he'd never seen me before. —Did you and Henry and Maitland cook that up together?

I stiffened and, without replying, stepped outside into the rain. I hadn't meant it to sound that way. Because it wasn't that way. But I'd said it, and Wes had taken it the only way he could. Maybe he was right.

Maybe being from Uptown New Orleans rubbed away your sensitivity until the only way you felt you could communicate was with a threat—or a bribe.

Back at the office, Marj had another surprise for me. A call from Jock Marvell, the best criminal lawyer in town. It seemed that Jock was representing Santorini Malaporte now. He wanted to go over the facts and talk the plea bargain with me.

Marj looked bemused. —I know what they say...

—What?

—The only way for a hood to hire a top-grade lawyer is to steal. But I checked and nothing big enough to cover Marvell's fees has gone down since Malaporte was released on bail.

—Then he called in all his credit with Kenny Amadeo, I told her. —Call Marvell's office. Tell him to come by. But give me a half-hour first. I've got to talk to... Dee-Dee.

Marj smiled. Nothing pleases her as much as having one of her absurd nicknames stick. Even for a little while.

I was lucky. Rat, a.k.a. Down and Dirty, was sitting behind his desk with a frozen yogurt, looking through a very large file.

—You've come, he said.

—You called?

—No. I just sent out mind pulses. They started when I saw this morning's paper.

—I don't think Wes and I are speaking.

—You got to give it to him. "The Hit Parade." That's nice. Maybe it only rings for the Geritol set, but it's nice.

—It has Maitland crawling around on his ceiling

—Is he eating flies yet?

—That article . . . it's the real thing, isn't it?

—What can I tell you, Dennie? I was in service in Germany when a lot of that stuff went down. But . . . what I know, what I hear . . . yeah, it's good stuff.

—Where do you think Wes is getting it?

Rat put down his empty yogurt cup and stared at me as if I'd lost my mind. —Santo Malaporte, where else?

I stared back at him. I suppose my expression wasn't much different from his. —That's . . . I mean, why would Malaporte . . . ?

Rat grinned, rubbed his fingers together.

—All right, he needed money, I admitted. —Bail, Marvell's fee . . . But he can get that from Kenny Amadeo, can't he?

—Amadeo wouldn't buy Santo a funeral. He might set him up for one—he may already have that in mind if he's seen the *Item*. I don't think he bought him bail, and I'm purely certain he's not renting Jock Marvell for him. Amadeo and Malaporte ain't that way about each other.

—Rat, are you sure?

—Sure I'm sure. Santo sold, baby. The only thing he had left to sell. Memories of the good old days with Franco Burnucci. Before the mob discovered Gucci shoes and we had girl assistant D.A.'s.

I didn't know if Rat was serious or not. I suspect he and Wes and all the others who've been around for years would just as soon D.A.'s were all former cops with night-school law degrees.

—Wes doesn't have that kind of money, I said uncertainly, remembering him visiting Malaporte in the holding cell.

Rat's smile came up like a winter sun. —How about Henry Holman? Reckon he might go a little bail?

Reckon he might drop a call on Marvell? For one hell of
a sweet story that doesn't implicate any of his Uptown
friends and neighbors?

—You tell me.

—Like Wes says. In a Shreveport second.

—Maitland's going to subpoena him. He can play
talk or time with Wes.

—Yeah. Maitland's just that dumb. Wes'll pop him
the finger, go to the hole, and sweat it out. Then he's
got two stories. "The Hit Parade" and D.A. Dick who
couldn't find his little business in the men's room.

—What's Maitland supposed to do, Rat?

—What I said at lunch, girl. Use Lazy Louie to nail
that wop bastard. Let Louie leave, and send Santo to
the slam.

By the time I'd walked back across the street to my
office, I was convinced Rat was right. He usually was.
But it was no use talking to John Maitland. Sometimes
it seemed he was working for the papers and television
stations instead of for the parish.

Jock Marvell was walking up and down looking out
the tall windows at dark autumn clouds moving in
from the northwest. —Winter's here, he smiled at me.

—Do you always say that when you get somewhere?

—Why, Denise, I've never gotten anywhere with
you.

Jock Marvell is another immigrant. He comes from
Houston, and he's never managed the transition from
boots to shoes. He wears dark conservative suits and a
Stetson that almost looks like an ordinary hat, but his
style would give him away even if he switched to formal wear. He's still single at thirty-five, and seems to
think of himself as a lady's man. Perhaps he is. He has
dark hair touched with gray, a high forehead, fine

brown eyes, and the things he can do with a jury would shame Laurence Olivier. Marj calls him 007. License to kill. Because he puts people back on the street who should have been born in prison and never let out.

Jock says he just plays the system, and he does. If people don't like the results, they should change the system. But if Jock Marvell played blackjack or chemin-de-fer the way he practices criminal law, there's not a casino in Las Vegas that would let him in the door.

If you could afford Jock's prices, you stood a lot better than a fifty-fifty chance of doing dirt and walking away. So far as I knew, he'd never lost a client to the Orleans Parish D.A.'s office. As I looked at him, admiring that warm Texas smile in spite of myself, I thought of what Wes had said about the criminal justice system. Crazy Lady.

I told Jock what I'd told Malaporte—what I had to say even though I didn't want to say it: if he'd testify against Louis Donovan, we'd let him plead attempted manslaughter. Five to ten. If the judge would go along, he'd do two to three with five probation. Jock shook his head.

—We'll do two, but no probation.

—What?

—When Santo comes out, he's got to work. To work, he's got to carry a gun. Probationers can't carry a gun.

—He's going to have to change his line of work, I said dryly.

—What's wrong with being a bodyguard or a security person? Jock asked, without the slightest sign of a grin.

I stared at the ceiling. He doesn't even need a jury to do it, does he?

—Jock, there's something else, I started to say, but then the grin broke through.

—Now we're going to talk about the story in the *Item*, right?

—You're always out front, aren't you?

—They don't pay squat for second place, Denise.

—I want affidavits on all the old business Malaporte is telling Wes Colvin. And his testimony if we get indictments and bring people to trial.

Jock nodded, considered, as if his next line wasn't pat. —I want a blanket immunity on the whole twenty-five years, and specific transactional immunity on every act he acknowledges taking part in or witnessing.

—A twenty-five-year blanket? Jock, you know I can't . . .

—And we want it all in the same package. The testimony against Donovan and the affidavits all go together. When Santo comes out, he doesn't want to look back.

I laughed. —He'll be looking back the rest of his life. The *Item* stories . . .

Jock smiled a little wider and shook his head. —Nope. When you sift through, it's all ancient history. None of it touches Amadeo, or Santo's former good buddies. Either they're dead already, the statute has run, or Santo doesn't give a damn.

—Let's talk Donovan alone.

—Sorry. My client tells me his memory drifts. This morning when we talked, he was humming "All or Nothing at All."

—So we do it your way, or listen to two hours of the fifth.

—That, Jock said, with no smile at all, —is it. I can't walk him through this. You've got a whole supermarket full of witnesses. But if you want what you say you want . . .

We broke it off then. I'd have to go back to Maitland

He'd scream and pound his desk and curse Marvell, and somewhere near the middle of the third act, between sobs and whispers, he'd probably agree to Jock's terms. The alternative was no sure conviction but Malaporte's . . . and that would look terrible on the front page of the *Item*. Crazy Lady.

Maitland surprised me. He did his histrionics, but then he said we'd wait till the rest of Wes's series was published, see who might be worth prosecuting out of the wealth of Malaporte's memoirs, and then make our decision. It seemed a reasonable enough idea.

—I don't suppose you could get advance copy from your friend at the paper? he asked me mordantly.

—We're not on very good terms just now, I told him.

—What about Henry Holman?

—He's not going to override his reporter. Why should he?

—The public interest, Maitland said.

—Henry's interests are . . . closely held. He'll have already read Wes's copy. No one he knows personally will be turning up.

Maitland looked surprised. —Of course not. We all know the same people.

—Of course . . . The public interest, I said, and left his office.

When the work day had ended and I'd driven home, the rain set in again, and the temperature dropped. Someone said there'd been talk of snow flurries in Shreveport, but no one in New Orleans paid any attention to that. I'd lived in New Orleans all my life. There'd never been enough for a snowball fight.

Winter in New Orleans means alternating cold wet gray days and even colder bright sunny days. Then one morning, usually close to Mardi Gras, certainly before Easter, spring creeps in overnight. But the winter months seem to stretch out like centuries.

It was hard to imagine them without Wes. Maybe we should talk. I entered the library and reached out for the phone, but just as I did, it rang. I didn't pick it up immediately. Let him wonder if I was home. On the fourth ring, I picked it up.

—Yes?

—Dennie sweet, it's Madeline.

—Oh, I said, disappointment likely showing in my voice. —Hello.

—As soon as I left the Pontchartrain, it occurred to me . . .

—Did we forget something?

—Of course we did. We didn't make a date for you to bring Wesley Colvin by. I would ask you for dinner, but I'm alone. René's in Lafayette tonight. How about brunch in the morning? It would be fun.

—Madeline, I'm sorry. I don't think Wes . . . I mean Wes and I . . .

—Something's wrong?

—We . . . seem to be having . . . a professional disagreement.

—Not about those silly articles in the *Item*? Daddy was by for coffee. He was crowing. It seems the *Washington Post* is interested in them.

—Everyone is . . . especially my boss.

—I can imagine. My God, I told Daddy, they make New Orleans seem like a slaughterhouse. Your young man must have a talent for twisted fiction.

—I almost wish that were so. But he has a source.

—Does he really? Who do you think could be telling all of it?

—I know who it is. Santorini Malaporte, the man we

arrested for trying to kill a used-car dealer's wife. He's probably at Wes's again tonight, telling him more loathsome stories.

Madeline was silent. I was afraid I knew what was passing through her mind. Wes isn't really our sort at all, is he, dearest? After a moment, I heard her let out her breath.

—Denise...

Her voice had an edge of urgency.

—Yes.

—I insist you come over by yourself for brunch tomorrow.

—Are you sure...?

—Yes, she answered a little sharply. Then she added bitterly, —We have plenty to talk about. It seems we're not awfully lucky with our men.

—Wes and I will get past this.

—I'm sure you will. And then the next one, and the one after that.

—Madeline, you make it sound as if...

—Isn't life more than... getting past one heartbreak after another? Isn't it supposed to be more? If I'd only thought of that before I married René. Denise, I spoke to him about the divorce. It was... awful.

Enough had happened that day. I didn't want to hear more of Madeline's problems just then. But I promised her I'd be there for brunch in the morning. Then I made excuses and hung up.

A few minutes before, staring out into the gloom, I'd thought I wanted to talk to Wes. But by the time I'd set the phone down, I'd changed my mind.

Saturday morning was bright and chill. I drove past Henry Holman's huge old Victorian mansion and parked in front of the house he had given Madeline for a wedding present, a more modern brick house a little farther up St. Charles, closer to Carrollton. There was a broad circular driveway out front, and the same dark young man I had seen with Madeline at St. Louis Cemetery, the St. Juste chauffeur I supposed, was polishing her Cadillac Fleetwood.

The sun was high, and the temperature had moderated. We'd be having brunch in the solarium, a confection of white wood, glass, faux bamboo furniture, and sunlight. She'd have asked Lulu, her housekeeper, to do her best things. Grits and grillades, perhaps. Crepes filled with scrambled eggs and crabmeat. And there would surely be pecan pie.

Madeline's newest maid met me at the door. She was an attractive young black girl who looked crisp and competent. Her name was Audrey, and she worked part-time to pay for her college courses in computer programming. She seemed surprised to see me.

—Miss Lemoyne . . . ?

—Yes. Good morning.

—Mr. René is out of town . . .

—I know.

—And Mrs. St. Juste isn't up yet.

—Are you sure?

—Yes, ma'am.

—Madeline's expecting me. She's probably getting dressed.

—I don't believe. I always run her bath first thing.

—Is Lulu here?

—No, ma'am. Lulu's off for the weekend.

I'd like to say I was puzzled, but I felt something more. Whatever emotional lapses Madeline might make, forgetting a social moment wasn't likely to be one of them. If she'd taken ill, she'd have phoned. Or had Audrey phone

—I think we'd better look in on Mrs. St. Juste, I said, wishing that I could smile and turn and walk back to my car and drive down to the Camellia Grill for an omelette.

—But...

—Audrey, it's necessary.

—Yes, ma'am.

We walked down the hall past the den, past the bright solarium filled with evergreen plants, and stopped in front of Madeline's bedroom door. I knocked and paused. Then knocked again.

—Madeline...I called out softly first. Then more loudly.

Audrey and I exchanged a glance. Her expression mirrored my own anxiety. Hesitantly, I opened the door.

She lay on a quilted bedspread, dressed in a long white silk gown and matching robe that touched the floor. Delicate white satin high-heeled boudoir slippers dangled from her bare feet. Her face was pale and her eyes seemed fixed on the crystal chandelier in the center of the ceiling, her expression one of mild puzzlement. Following her glance, I looked up, too. Then back down quickly as I realized that her eyes were dull, unmoving, and there was a medallion of bright blood circled around a darker place in the left center of her breast, with rills like scarlet ribbons running from it to nest in the gown's fresh white lace.

CHAPTER
5

O h, sweet Jesus, Audrey cried out.
   I took her by the shoulders and turned her around, pushing her back out into the hall.

—I want you to go and sit in the kitchen, Audrey. No, the library. There's a decanter of brandy on the end of the library table. Pour two glasses.

—Yes, ma'am. Shouldn't I call a doctor?

—No. Just wait there.

She was halfway down the hall before her tears and sobs began. I turned back into the room, and looked at Madeline again. The first time had been nothing more than an image, the kind of shimmering uncertain picture that can pass through a nasty dream. This time, it was what we call . . . real. I saw Madeline's carefully manicured hands lying strengthless on the soft coverlet. She wore only her wedding ring. I touched her wrist, searching with no hope for the least sign of a pulse, but pulled my hand away quickly. The chill of her flesh was the certain sign of death.

I started to lean over and close her eyes, but it occurred to me that I shouldn't. Whatever had happened, the police would want what Rat Trapp called a clean scene. I stepped back, and only then realized that tears were running down my cheeks.

I numbly wiped them away as I walked down the hallway, wondering why I wasn't screaming—or at least as moved as Audrey, whose sobs and snufflings I could hear coming from the library. God knows it wasn't that I didn't love Madeline, but I had become almost inured to seeing people I loved dead. My grandfather, my father. Somehow I had thought it was behind me, over with. That had been foolish. If you live long enough, you'll see whole generations of the city die, person by person. You're going to see death like this until you're done with life yourself.

When I phoned Rat he was still at his apartment down St. Charles Avenue eight or ten blocks away. He listened without saying anything, and told me he'd be right there.

I'd thrown down a Courvoisier and was sitting across the leather-topped library table from Audrey when it struck me. Oh, Christ, Rat would call Tulane and Broad. He'd want his forensic people here as quickly as possible. Which meant in a matter of minutes, police cars would be flashing their lights and roaring through traffic signals along St. Charles. Past Henry Holman's house. Perhaps he'd hear them squeal to a stop and step outside to check if something awful had befallen a neighbor, and see . . .

I was up on my feet and out the front door, calling back to Audrey.

—Tell him I'm at Henry Holman's house. He'll understand.

Henry came to the door in old tattered wine-colored

sweater Madeline had knitted him when she was still attending Sacred Heart Academy.

—Well, what's this? Answer to an old man's day-dreaming?

I couldn't answer. I'd used the last of my breath, the last of my control, to run the short block and a half between Madeline's house and his.

—Uncle Henry, I finally choked out, —something terrible has...

—Come on in, baby. We'll talk about it. Wes has his good points and his bad. But I'm well studied in the turnings and twistings of the redneck soul.

As he closed the door behind us, I heard a police siren far away. It was coming down St. Charles at incredible speed.

Henry sat in his worn leather chair for a long time without saying anything. The drapes were drawn closed, and the room was in deep shadow except for a knife-edge of sunlight that cut between them here and there. One of the shafts struck his hand as it lay on the chair's armrest. The thick fingers were splayed, the wrist limp. Then, slowly, I saw the fingers come together to form a fist, the knuckles white. His voice, when it came, was hoarse and low. Not the voice of an old man, but of one who was very tired.

—I hadn't ought to have lived this long, he said slowly. —Wasn't any need. My worst enemy, I wouldn't wish it on him to live for... this.

—Uncle Henry, please... let me get you something.

—That would be nice. There's a bottle of Jack Daniel's in the cupboard. You want to bring two glasses.

—I had a glass of brandy before I came.

—Good. You bring the glasses anyhow.

I brought back the bottle and one glass. My hands trembled as I poured him perhaps an inch. He smiled up at me from the shadows, and I could see there were rills of tears running down his red beefy cheeks. He took the bottle from me and poured the cocktail glass half full.

—It's not a two-finger pain, honey.

—Uncle Henry, I called Rat Trapp.

—Trapp? The big nigra detective. Wes Colvin's buddy.

—Mine, too.

—I know him. We've . . . dealt.

—He should be there now. I have to get back. Are you coming with me?

Henry stood up, shaking his head, the tears flowing freely now.

—No, Dennie, you go on. I'll want to change first. My little girl wouldn't want me over there looking like this.

He shuffled out of the study into the hall and up the stairs looking very tired. I wanted to stay with him, but I walked to the front door, opened it, took a deep breath, and pulled it to behind me.

Rat was in the den, leaning against a beautiful old Empire desk that René had always treasured. Madeline had given it to him as an anniversary gift long ago. For an instant, I hardly recognized Rat. I'd never seen him in a jogging suit before. Behind him, French doors opened onto a walled flagstone courtyard at the back of the house. Even in winter, the luxurious evergreen plants there gave it the look of a corner in the tropics somewhere. The sunlight was almost blinding as it struck the faded old brick of the wall opposite and lost itself among the shrubs and bushes. I noticed that one of the panes was broken at the level of the handle. The Oriental rug was covered with glass.

—Anybody been in here, Dennie?

—No. I mean, I don't know. I didn't come in. I doubt Audrey did.

—I asked. She didn't. So . . .

He turned his upper body and gestured into the darkness across the room. Over there, René's gun cabinet, as large as an armoire, stood with one glass-paneled door open.

—Lot of B and E around here the last month or so, Rat said after a long moment.

—I know. I think of it every time I'm home alone at night.

—See, what it looks like is, we've got a doper or some project punk saw him a nice easy house. Lots of glass doors, lots of rooms. Burglar bars front only. He busted in through that French door, thinking nobody was here. Took what he wanted from the gun locker, looked all around . . .

For the first time, I noticed that the pictures on the wall were askew, that the rug had been pulled away from the walls.

—Looking for a safe? I asked.

—Or whatever.

Rat moved away from the desk. The drawers his legs had been hiding were pulled out. Papers were strewn on the floor.

—This ought to have been it, Rat said. —I mean this room. But it wasn't. Unless he wanted to go out with an armload of guns, wasn't anything in here would buy him a double bag, or a ticket to L.A., or whatever he was looking to fund.

Rat stepped into the hall like a sleepwalker, his eyes still narrow, lips tight. I knew what he was doing. He was walking in the burglar's shoes. You get in their heads, he'd told me once. You occupy their minds. You live with them till you find them.

We were walking down the hall then, toward Madeline's bedroom. The officers and lab people who had been standing in the hallway pressed up against the wall. They knew Rat's ways and respected them. No one interfered with him, no one questioned him. We had almost reached the bedroom door when I heard Henry's voice behind us.

—Denise . . .

—Wait, I told Rat. —It's Henry . . .

—Ah, Rat said, without breaking his concentration. He didn't turn to meet Henry. He walked on to the bedroom, leaving me to return to the foyer, take Henry's hand, hug him.

He was dressed in a dark suit, his scant hair still glistening from the water he had used to comb it back. His mouth was a jagged unsteady slit, and his eyes were dark and anguished. He had already done his first crying. That was part of the reason he'd waited behind.

—Jacoby, I heard Rat's voice saying in the bedroom, —you got what you need?

I couldn't make out the mumbled response.

—Then cover the lady up, Rat said, his voice edgy, much lower. —She ain't part of the furniture, goddamnit.

Henry was staring past me, and I don't think he even heard. Rat stepped into the hallway again, his bulk blocking the way into the bedroom.

—Mr. Holman, he said, —my condolences.

—My daughter's . . . in there?

Rat nodded. —It's up to you. Miss Lemoyne has identified your daughter for me. There's nothing you need to do.

For a long moment Henry didn't answer. I thought that his mind had wandered. He didn't seem to hear. Finally he nodded at Rat.

—I want to see her. When they're done, before the ambulance people . . .

Rat stepped aside. —I got certain questions, you understand. But they don't have to come now.

—Oh yeah they do, Henry said, his voice stronger, rougher, like the grit of an emery board. —Oh yeah . . . questions . . .

He stepped past Rat into the bedroom. Someone had opened the drapes. The sunlight through the window almost hurt my eyes. One of Rat's people had placed a silk comforter from the closet over Madeline. Only her right arm remained uncovered. Henry knelt beside the bed, taking her small hand, wrapping it in both of his so that it vanished as he leaned down over her. It seemed a long time before he reached up and drew back the edge of the comforter.

Someone—Rat, most likely—had closed her eyes, and nothing in her expression suggested fear or unhappiness. Her hair was perfectly smooth and ordered, her makeup flawless. Her lips were closed in what seemed like the faintest of smiles. Madeline looked as if she had passed from her troubles into the serenity of a dreamless sleep. The death I had seen before was not so kind.

Henry's hand started to pull the comforter down farther.

—You don't want to do that, I said.

He looked up at me almost in surprise. —No, he said, —I don't need to do that.

He leaned over and kissed her forehead, her cheek. Then he replaced the comforter and turned to us.

—I'm ready for your questions now, Captain, Henry said quietly.

Rat stepped across to Madeline's Italian secretary desk. I saw a leather-bound volume that looked like a diary lying open on top, but Rat reached below the desktop and drew out one of the drawers.

—Forced. Nice smooth job. Just a couple of marks by the lock.

—Jesus, Henry said, shaking his head from side to side as if there was something he wanted to deny.

—She kept something in here? Rat asked. —If so, it's gone. Just an empty drawer. Not even a piece of paper.

—She... A few months ago, Maddie inherited her momma's jewelry. I told her to put it in her safe-deposit box down at the Whitney Bank. She told me just now she wanted it close. Said when she took it out and looked at it, she could see her momma wearing it again.

He lost his control for a moment. I took his arm, and he covered my hand with his, patting it.

—It's all right, baby. It's just... if somebody killed her for those damned trinkets I gave her momma forty years ago...

—This wasn't no B and E, Mr. Holman, Rat said abruptly. —This was somebody wanted me to *think* it was burglary.

—How can you be so sure?

Rat gestured for us to follow him down the hall to the den. He pushed the French door closed, then pointed down to the floor where the glass from the shattered pane lay scattered.

—What's it tell you? he asked.

Henry and I exchanged confused glances.

—If I'm out, and break the glass coming in, where's

it gonna fall? Rat asked. He squatted and stabbed at the floor just under the door handle, then dragged his finger across the rug for ten or twelve inches. When he stopped his finger, it was still short of where the pattern of broken window glass began.

—Fucking door was *open* when they broke that glass.

He opened the door slowly until the bottom was an inch or two from where the broken glass lay. I could sense that he was right. The door had been open wide enough to allow anyone to pass through when the glass was broken.

Rat whistled loudly. A uniformed police officer appeared in the doorway to the den.

—You get all the servants lined up for me, hear? That little maid and... He turned back to us. —Is there a gardener, butler?

—A chauffeur, I said.

—The yardman's just day help, Henry put in. —But Lulu, the housekeeper... she's usually here. Not weekends though.

—I'll talk to all of 'em. Somebody's jerking us around.

—You should go home now, Uncle Henry. Get some rest.

Henry was on his feet then, and the three of us walked back to the foyer. I could see the TV remote truck outside through the panels of beveled glass on either side of the door. A TV cameraman was focusing on the house under the direction of a woman reporter who stood just behind him, naming angles.

—In the old days, Rat almost whispered, —a man could lay dead for hours before the buzzards found him. It'd be best if Mr. Holman went out the back and around the block. Even if he is an old newspaperman.

Rat ordered one of his men to see Henry home. I followed Rat into the library where Madeline's household help were waiting.

Rat looked from Audrey to the chauffeur. He stood with his cap in his hand, as if he thought he'd been called in to drive Madeline somewhere. He was young, tall, with good shoulders, large hands, and dark wavy hair. His eyes were dark and set wide apart. He had no accent that I could notice, and yet I was sure he was from another country.

—You got a name?

—Mario. Truxillo.

—You stay around here?

—There's a garage apartment out back.

—You got a key to the main house?

—No. I wouldn't need that. When nobody's home, it's 'cause I'm driving them somewhere.

Rat turned to Audrey and went through all the questions I'd have asked, with a few curves thrown in. He wanted to know where Audrey's boyfriend stayed. Did he have a record? She said he was in the Marines. Stationed at some embassy in Central America. Audrey had only come on duty at nine that morning. She'd let herself in with her key. There was nothing unusual in Madeline's still being asleep—or in René's being gone. That was the way Saturdays seemed to go at the St. Juste house.

Then Rat looked back at Madeline's driver. How often did Mario Truxillo have people in? Who were they? Where could they be found?

—Look, Truxillo said at last, —aren't you supposed to read us rights or something?

—If I was taking you in, I would. You want to go downtown and talk a while there?

—No, but I want to know if I'm a suspect. Like, I was off last night. I wasn't here. If I'm gonna need an alibi...

—You'd like to get started building one.

—I never said that.

—Right. You never did.

Truxillo had come to New Orleans from Florida last year. Until six or seven months ago he had worked for a package delivery service but got tired of fighting downtown traffic. He'd answered an ad in the *Item* for a driver and handyman, was hired by Mrs. St. Juste, and worked for her ever since.

—And that's all I got to say, Truxillo told Rat sullenly.

—Yeah?

—You got anymore questions, I want a lawyer.

—Hey, now... You *do* want to go downtown, don't you?

—No, but...

Rat turned to one of the uniformed policemen who still stood in the background.

—Fontenot, why don't you take Mr. Truxillo to Central Lockup and make him comfortable. Let him call a lawyer right off.

—Wait a minute, Truxillo began.

Rat grinned as Fontenot came up and took Truxillo's arm. He stared at Rat for a moment, then shrugged and turned away, heading for the door with Fontenot just behind him.

—Oh, yeah, Fontenot. Be sure and read him his rights. He's been looking forward to that.

—Do you think...? I started.

—Counselor, it's not even close to thinking time yet.

—I don't understand...

Rat silenced me with a look, then gestured for Audrey to leave the room.

—This is the first case we're looking at together—starting from scratch, right? he said when she was gone.

—Yes.

—Then you're gonna get your first look at Gonzo police work.

—Gonzo . . . police . . .

—If it don't fall open in front of you so you can close it down with an arrest, shake up everybody. Look mean and stir the pot. See, I'm gonna find out if little Audrey's Marine boyfriend is in El Quackador or wherever. Or is he on leave? She got brothers? A stepfather? What kind of shit are they into? What did Mario do with that nice hair and long lashes over in Fort Lauderdale? Did he leave tracks? Is he in trouble over there—with cops or anybody else? I want to know a whole lot about Lulu, too. She ever have a son went to prison?

—Gonzo or gizmo, you're on the wrong track with Lulu. She's been with the St. Justes for as long as I can remember . . . over twenty years at least. And she was with the Holmans before that.

—Fine. Maybe I'm off base there. But I like to throw *all* the pieces up in the air. When everybody's got the jitters, *then* I go to thinking. See, if I'm thinking and the killer's thinking, he's got an edge on me. He knows what happened. I don't. But if I can shake him up . . .

—He'll stop thinking.

—Hard to think if it looks like a big mean spook cop is fixing to chaw off your leg.

—Rat, you're . . . unconventional.

He smiled and spread his hands. —See, nobody ever invited me to the conventions.

I was telling Rat I'd like to break the news to Lulu before he questioned her when another thought struck me.

—Good God, I said. —We haven't even tried to get in touch with René . . . Madeline's husband.

—Mr. St. Juste? Audrey told me she reckoned he'd be in later today. Seems he stays overnight in Lafayette on Fridays. Wouldn't be easy to run him down on the road.

—Still . . . if he turned on his car radio . . .

—I'll call the state police. You don't have a license number for him, do you?

—No. Sorry.

—No matter. We'll pull it out of the computer. Matter of fact, I'd as soon we *did* find him on the road. Just to see what he's been up to.

—Rat, you're not going to gonzo René St. Juste?

—Oh, honey, you missing the soul of the thing. I just thrash around a lot. People gonzo themselves.

—They do at that, don't they?

I started toward the kitchen door intending to circle around to my car parked out on the street. I wanted to get to Lulu Washington before she saw the TV news. —I'll catch up with you later, I called back to Rat.

—Better charge your jet-pack, baby. I'm gonna put this one away fast.

Just then the front door opened. One of the uniformed officers backed in, trying to keep reporters and cameramen outside. From somewhere among them I saw a man emerge. He was dressed in a light gray tweed jacket and dark blue slacks. He looked dazed and very tired. Rat stepped forward to ask just who he was, but the intruder saw me and, instead of answering, called out.

—Denise, what in God's name is happening?

As he started toward me, Rat put one hand on his arm as if to hold him back.

—Rat, it's all right. This is René St. Juste

CHAPTER

6

What's happened? A burglary? But why are there so many police?

I glanced at Rat, but he shook his head. He didn't want me to say anything.

—I'm Ralph Trapp, Mr. St. Juste. You weren't home last night?

—No, no . . . I go to my Lafayette office on Fridays. I stay at the Tidewater Motel overnight. Look, tell me what's happened. How much did they get?

—We can't say about that, Mr. St. Juste. Maybe some jewelry.

—That damned stuff of Madeline's mother? I told her to take it down to the bank, but she . . .

René paused, apparently realizing for the first time that Madeline wasn't among the people crowding the foyer. He turned his head down the hall in the direction of the bedroom.

—Where is she? he asked. —Where's Madeline?

—Mr. St. Juste . . . Rat started, but that time I shook my head. He shrugged and fell silent.

I took René's arm and pulled him down the hall toward the den. Rat started to follow, but then drew back.

—Denise, what are all these people doing here? There are newspeople outside. For God's sake, why would a burglary . . .

I think it was his own words, the sound of them rather than whatever expression I must have had on my face that pulled him up short. René's dark tanned face seemed to go slack, his eyes widened.

—Madeline . . . Has something happened to her?

—Someone shot her, René. She's . . .

—Dead? Not dead . . . for God's sake . . .

I didn't answer. I didn't even nod. René sat down heavily in a chair at the near side of his desk. Expressionless, he stared out the door of the study into the pale sunlight. For a moment I watched him. I wanted to know what I couldn't possibly know. What was he feeling? I wouldn't have expected him to break down, to lose his control. He hadn't been reared for that.

Southern men rarely show the full depth of their feelings. It has been bred out of them, Wes told me once. It had to be. In the old days, there had been so many things a country man might encounter that would break his heart. Only very wealthy city people could afford the full range of their emotions, because they were so rarely called upon to express them. René's shoulders didn't move. I could hear no sound from him at all. Then it struck me that I was being crude, that my curiosity had no business here. Gonzo investigation wasn't my specialty. I stepped into the hall and left René to feel whatever he might be feeling.

Back in the foyer, Rat studied me a moment then asked, —What's on your mind? What's warting you?

—I think ... I started to say, then fell silent.

Rat frowned, took hold of my hand.

—Denise, I know you're hurting, and I know how many ties and old times run between you and these folks. But this is work, honey. See, if it was my own momma they took away, it's still work.

I nodded. Why did he have to say that to me? No, why had I given him reason to feel he had to say that to me?

—I think, whatever he tells you, you should check René's story ... very carefully.

Rat nodded. —Love, you can bet the pool and hot tub on that. When he come through the door, I thought, that's one slick-looking dude. Reckon what he's got hid out.

He paused, then gave me a quick sharp look. —Go on.

—What ...?

—Tell me why I'm gonna look him over from asshole to appetite.

—Rat ...

—Sorry. Go on. Tell me.

—Ordinarily, I wouldn't even think it was worth ...

—Dennie ...

—I had lunch with Madeline two days ago at the Caribbean Room.

—All right. Youall saw each other regularly, didn't you?

—Not so much in the last several years ... but ... yes.

—So you had lunch ...

—Madeline was very unhappy. She said ... she felt

René didn't love her anymore, that he was just staying with her because of the money.

Rat listened thoughtfully, nodding as I talked.

—I thought he had money.

—Not in the beginning, I said. —And maybe not now. He deals in oil leases. Henry Holman's contacts and Madeline's money got him started. It went beautifully for a long time. But recently. . .

—Those camel jockeys in the Mideast lost control of the sweetest scam in history.

—I don't know if Madeline had any real reason to say those things about him.

—Yeah, well, a woman her age . . . It can get to looking all downhill. Is that what you mean?

I nodded silently, wondering why I was cutting, editing what Madeline had told me. I felt dumb and dishonest. It must have shown. Rat's eyes never wavered from my face.

—That's everything material that was said?

—We talked about . . . that damned silly case I got involved with at Schwegmann's Supermarket.

—And?

—She . . . Madeline said . . . she wondered if René might not do the same thing to her.

Rat's expression never changed, but his voice was suddenly cool.

—That's material. I'd like a signed statement covering whatever passed between you and Madeline St. Juste at that last meal in the Caribbean Room. I want the facts of what was said, and I want your impressions, too. I'd like it first thing Monday if you can manage that.

—All right. You'll have it an hour after I get to the office.

—That will be just fine, Rat said. Then he left for

Central Lockup to catch the coroner's report as soon as it was available, and to question Mario Truxillo. He said he'd be back to question René later. I should tell him to keep himself available.

The foyer emptied quickly as the police filed out after Rat. My personal and professional feelings were so confused that I didn't want to talk to René. I felt as if I'd betrayed a dear and close friend in telling Rat what I had. But, I told myself, Maitland would surely assign another prosecutor to this case and then I'd be no more than a witness, one of the mourners, a family friend. There was no excuse for my failing to offer René support.

He sat in the same posture I'd left him a few minutes before. I stood at the door silently until he looked up.

—Have they gone?

—What can I get for you? Coffee, a drink?

René didn't answer. He had been crying. I was sure of it. He lifted his eyes to the open French doors that remained just the way Rat had left them. The sun was still bright in the courtyard outside, but a chill breeze ruffled the drapes. René shivered as I walked over and closed the door.

—There's still the broken pane, I said. —You could tape a piece of pasteboard over it. Shall I ask Audrey to clean up the glass?

—The police . . .

—They've photographed and dusted in here.

He nodded, eyes still fixed on the brightness of the courtyard.

—I could use a drink, Dennie.

As I started for the library to get the brandy, René rose and followed. We walked down the hall side by side, René's arm around me.

As we stood at the carved mahogany bar over our

drinks, I explained what Rat thought had happened, how I came to be there.

—Jesus, he said as I finished and poured another brandy. —If I'd taken the interstate home, I would have found her. But I drove the long way from Lafayette. Through the bayou country, U.S. Ninety.

—You weren't in a hurry to get home?

He glanced at me as I passed him the drink. For an instant, it seemed to me he looked afraid.

—Autumn, he said softly, as if he hadn't heard my question. —Squirrel hunters in woods where the leaves have fallen. Even driving I could hear the shotguns . . .

René's voice fell off. He threw down the brandy.

—I was happy then, he said wistfully. —Really happy.

—Driving home this morning?

—Yes. And before. When I was young.

—Strange . . .

—What?

—I never thought of you as a hunter.

He laughed without humor. —It was a long time ago . . . out in the parish. I've got to look for those . . . all the good memories.

—Does it take looking? Were there so few? I don't remember it that way.

He glanced at me sharply. As if he were wondering whether I was indulging in therapy or investigation. René seemed satisfied with what he saw in my face. He reached across the bar for the bottle of Remy Martin and poured another drink.

—You were just a girl, he said, his voice thin, distracted. —It wasn't always good around here. Years ago, Madeline and I stopped talking about anything important. All the years we spent together, I never knew her.

He carried the bottle of brandy across the room, put his glass down, and stared at the dark ebony wood and tooled black leather of the library table without seeing it.

—Jesus, now . . . I'll never know her, will I?

René's lips trembled. He covered his mouth with a big fist, strong fingers moving across his cheeks.

—All those years . . . like the world's longest one-night stand. Two people who don't know each other. Doing whatever they do because they're . . . there.

—René, for God's sake . . .

—Maybe you should go, Denise. I'm going to drink the rest of this brandy. Then I'm going to find something else. Bourbon, peach cordial, wine vinegar . . . I don't give a damn. My own private wake. After that, the goddamned town will flood in. All Uptown New Orleans . . .

—People will want to help, I said.

—No one here helps anyone. They just want to see one another in pain. They want to touch the pain with their eyes, their ears. It makes them feel alive. . . .

I felt my breath catch in my throat. Why was René saying those things? It sounded as if he'd been talking to Wes.

—But there's nobody alive in this graveyard of a town except the niggers and poor whites . . . and a handful of aliens like me. When you move Uptown, they ought to have a ceremony. How about a funeral?

He sat down heavily, and poured more brandy. He poured too rapidly. Some of it splashed out of the glass and onto the dark wood of the table, onto the gilded leather. René touched it with his finger, stared at the spreading liquor curiously.

—Hundred percent casualties. Nobody alive . . . Not even Madeline . . .

He lay his arm on the table's surface and lowered his head to rest on it. I reached out my hand, then drew it back. René didn't answer when I said goodbye. He hadn't lifted his head from the table as I walked through the foyer and closed the front door quietly behind me.

I drove across town then to Lulu Washington's. I would not likely beat the awful news to her door, but I could try to ease the anguish of it for her.

As I drove, I remembered that Lulu had made my first communion veil. My father and grandfather had gone to Madeline, supposing somehow that a little girl's first communion was a feminine venture, and that, after all, since Madeline had been my godmother, the duty properly fell to her.

Madeline had cheerfully taken over the arrangements. She had bought me a ruffled white organdy dress, but decided all the veils at Maison Blanche were tacky. She had drafted Lulu who, years before, had worked as a seamstress for Madeline's mother. Lulu had worked at night after her day's labor was done and sewed a light frothy creation that was the envy of my classmates at St. Cecilia's School.

As I parked in front of Lulu's old faded double house in Mid-city, I found that I was crying. Really crying for the first time for Madeline, for René, for Lulu, for the loving times past.

I got myself together, fixed my makeup, and walked up the cracked wooden steps to the door. An elderly black woman answered my knock. For a moment, I thought it was Lulu.

—Lulu . . . no, it's Clio, isn't it?

—Yes ma'am. And you're . . . Lord, Miss Denise . . . She pushed open the screen door, and we hugged.

—It's been a long time.

—It has that.

—I have to see Lulu. Is she here?

Clio nodded, dry-eyed, expressionless. As if no news that one could bring was likely to cause her pain or make her cry. As if she were beyond both.

—You come about Miz St. Juste, didn't you?

I nodded. I was too late, but I hoped Henry had thought to call. Lulu had worked for him and Madeline's mother since she was a young girl. After Madeline had married she had been unhappy with the help she could find, and Henry had asked Lulu to go with the St. Justes. You raised the girl, Henry had told her. You ought to see it through.

—I'll see if she can come out, Miss Denise.

As I waited, I looked around the room. The furnishings were very old, worn, the upholstery bare on the arms of Victorian chairs, the seats of a dainty old sofa trimmed in carved wood. On one wall was a colored lithograph of the Immaculate Heart of Mary. Just opposite, another of the Sacred Heart. In a corner, almost out of sight, was an old oak prie-Dieu with a large missal almost the size of a Mass book on it. Dozens of framed pictures of blacks I didn't know lined the mantel. Some of the pictures were very old, probably reproductions of tintypes made around the turn of the century. The people in them were starched and upright and unsmiling, the men wearing odd round collars that had not been worn in sixty years, the women dressed in fussy floor-length gowns. The fireplace was small, framed by metal stamped with the design of two dancing women in classical costumes, enwreathed by vines of laurel or some such. Pieces of coal pulsed red and blue and autumn yellow in it.

Clio brought Lulu in, both her hands under her sister's arm. It had not been long since I last saw Lulu, but if we had passed on the street, I wouldn't have recognized her.

Her white hair was invisible under an old nylon stocking folded into a kind of skullcap. Her face was as expressionless as Clio's, and she walked slowly, tentatively, like an old woman. But it was her eyes that shocked me. Except for their occasional movement, they seemed the eyes of someone dead.

Clio helped her sit down in a slatback rocker near the hearth, then moved away to sit on the sofa with her hands folded. Lulu quietly began to rock. So far she had not even acknowledged my presence. After what seemed a long time, she looked over at me, and I heard her sigh.

—Nothing gonna go right, ain't no need of hoping it will. 'Cause it won't. Go long for some time, maybe for years. But it all come down at the end. Going right is just the look of a thing before it come down on you.

—Lulu, I'm so sorry. You know how I loved her.

Lulu nodded and rocked.

—Everybody love her, Lulu started. She stopped rocking abruptly and looked over at me, those dead eyes almost sly, some hint of malignant life rousing in them. —Almost everybody.

Then she began again, eyes fixed on the barely visible flames that licked at the chunks of coal in the fireplace.

—Her momma was always sickly. Uptown woman. Liked a levee or a soirée. Liked champagne and oysters. Come to where she always going one bright place or another when Mr. Holman took over the newspaper.

Lulu shook her head, in grief and covert outrage over shames perpetrated half a century ago.

—Wasn't never time for the child. Never even wanted the child. Poor little girl alone day in, day out. Daddy loved her, but a man got to do what men do. Give her an afternoon at Audubon or pony ride out to City Park. One birthday, he took her to Pontchartrain Park. Rode the whip or whatever they called it. Rode the merry-go-round. Even that day, her momma had a headache. Been out to three in the morning having a high time. Mr. Holman felt awful, too. But he got up and took the child. Years on, she told me she thought she must be ugly and bad, 'cause nobody truly love her but me. Jesus, sweet Jesus. Nobody but me.

I felt as if I stood on the brink of an archaeological dig, watching a distant past unfurling out of the blank, dusty, lifeless earth. Only it wasn't an unspeakably ancient Sumerian past, or some moment from an un-recollected Egyptian past. It was mine as much as Madeline's. It made me understand why she would care so much for a little girl without a mother—another one whose father had so many things to do.

It answered a question I had always held in the old time of my mind but never concretely asked even of myself. Why had Madeline been my godmother—rather than Henry Holman's proper Uptown Catholic wife? It must have been another headache, another bad day, the day that I was baptized. But Madeline had been grown then, a proper young lady in her twenties. She had stepped in smoothly for her mother. I wondered if we might have been closer if grandfather had told me, if I had realized.

—Lulu, you know I work for the district attorney's office now.

—Miss Madeline told me. Said you took over from your daddy.

I felt the blood rising in my cheeks. I had taken nothing from my father, wanted nothing from him but my own release.

—Is there anything you can tell me?

—Tell you?

—I know you weren't there when it...happened. But if you saw anyone loitering outside the house during the week...anything...

She shook her head as she rocked, her hands twisted tightly, one within the other.

—No, she said almost dreamily. —I can't hardly hear, my eyes no good. What do I know? Jesus, Mary, and Joseph...she didn't have nobody but me...

She fell silent then, and I could see that she was weeping.

For some reason, I glanced over at Clio. She seemed to have come to life as we sat there. She was perched on the edge of the sofa as if my next words, my next question, could somehow be crucial. But I had no next question. It seemed pointless to press Lulu further, to interfere with her memories, with her finding the pathways in her own soul to come to terms with losing Madeline.

As Clio held open the door for me, I tried to grasp what it was about her expression, her inchoate mood, that surprised and troubled me.

I had driven halfway home in the chill bright fading afternoon before it came to me. Clio had been terribly afraid.

When I reached the old house on State Street, it was twilight. The sun was gone, and the sky had a hard cold look about it. I parked the car under the sally port beside the house and walked around to the front. In the twilight, I could see that someone was sitting on the steps. I stopped for a moment. A burglar or mug-

ger? One of the drunks from down on Camp Street
who wandered into Uptown just to see what it was like
on the other side of the world?

—I tried to call you when it came in on the police
radio, the figure said, speaking no louder than if I were
sitting on the steps beside him. —I drove up to Henry's
place, but you weren't there. He didn't know where
you'd have gone. I was worried.

I went into Wes's arms as if we'd been parted by a
war, away from one another for years. It didn't matter
to either of us who had been wrong. We both knew
what was right.

Inside, we sat by a fire Wes made. I didn't even
bother turning on the central heat. The library was
warm, and the long dark halls and empty rooms all
around us melted away in the shadows. We drank
brandy and watched the flames as they broke free of
the wood and spiraled upward.

—I came to tell you...we ought to be together.
When I heard your friend Madeline was dead, I
thought...what if you'd walked in just as...

—I thought she'd slept late. I found her lying on her
bed, I heard myself saying in a strange dreamy de-
tached voice. —She looked lovely. Except for this place
on her chest, a little blood...

—Don't do that, Dennie. Put it out of mind.

Wes pulled me close, and we kissed for a long time.
But instead of making me happy, the kiss seemed to
break my emotions free. I lay in his arms crying.

—Jesus, I'll have to improve my style, he said.

I just cried harder. Remembering Madeline alive and
well and happy years ago. Wondering if I'd made a terrible mistake, added to René's grief, by telling Rat
something of what had passed between Madeline and
me before she died.

—Come on, Wes said, rising to his feet, pulling me along with him.

—Where?

—Get some stuff.

—But . . .

—We'll drive out to Alonso's and have stuffed crab. Then home to my place for the night.

—Wes . . .

—This house is getting to you. I don't want you here alone. Too many memories, most of them bad.

He waved his arms around at the darkness.

—Look at it. Ten feet from the fire, and it's like being in one of those mausoleums. Cold, clammy, empty.

—Your apartment is warmer?

Wes put his hand over his heart.

—I swear to God. Twenty thousand redneck thermal units. Oh, baby, you'll sweat. I'll make you sweat.

—I'll bet.

I woke up in the small hours of the night, somewhere around 2 or 3 A.M. I thought I'd heard someone call out to me.

I sat bold upright, disoriented and frightened for a moment. Then I realized I was in Wes's bed, as warm as he had promised I'd be. The radio was playing very low. One of those stations that plays nothing but old music. A theme I remembered from when I was very young, stated over and over again in the violins, a piano playing in front. Then I remembered the name: "Love in Every Room."

By the faint moonlight coming through the glass courtyard door, I could see him beside me, one arm twisted around a pillow. His straight hair was over his eyes, and even in sleep his expression was serious and ironic all at once. I watched him for a long while, feeling his warm body, close to mine.

I wondered if he was hunting or fishing in his dream, or investigating, digging, and delving for the truth, or perhaps making love to me. As I lay down again, he turned, still sleeping, and pulled me closer with both arms, kissing my shoulders, my arms, my face, and then I knew.

CHAPTER

7

The sound of rain on the flagstones of the courtyard awoke me. I opened my eyes from dreamless sleep and looked outside. It was almost nine in the morning, but it was twilight out there. The rain had started to fall in wind-twisted sheets once more, rattling the glass doors, shaking the leafless mimosa just outside. I shivered under the covers.

Wes was pouring coffee into two enormous mugs. One had his birth sign, the other mine. Scorpio and Leo. The smell of the coffee brought me around. Wes came back to bed and pulled the blanket up to his chin.

—I'm glad you stayed the night. You don't look so good.

—That's a nasty thing to say. I just woke up, and . . .

—You're gorgeous. I mean you look like you've been . . .

—I know what you mean.

—Thinking about Madeline St. Juste.

—And René St. Juste and Lulu Washington and Henry Holman. And God knows who else is hurting.

—I've seen it a lot. Some dumb bastard needs a fix or a ticket to Chicago. He's stupid and clumsy, and he slaughters somebody for fifty bucks and change. Then the waves of pain and loss start to spread. Maybe they catch him, convict him . . . and give him a few years . . .

Wes laughed, not trying to mask the bitterness.

—I wonder how many of the victims would have been ready to settle for that same ten years in prison— just to stay alive.

—Rat's sure it was no simple B and E, I said. —The person who shot Madeline just tried to make it look that way. Pass me the phone, please . . .

—You want the weather forecast? Rain and colder. This year we get snow. Any day now . . .

—That's absurd. The phone, please . . .

I dialed and waited. Then Rat answered.

—Uhhh . . .

—I'm too early.

—No. It's not sleep. I just came in from running around Audubon Park. I'm trying to get my breath back.

—You went jogging this morning? Have you looked outside?

—Love, I just said: I *been* outside. Colder than a honky's heart. Wetter than a . . .

—I could call back later.

—It's all right. I guess you want to know . . . Mario got down to the lockup and went dumb.

—What?

—There's nothing on him here, so we've got his prints working through the FBI computer. We checked out his little place back of the St. Juste house. Nothing.

It was clean. But I'm gonna stay on this ass till I know why he stopped talking.

—Did you get him a lawyer?

—When he got downtown, he never asked. He just sat there with his arms folded.

—What are you going to do?

—Soon as I get some coffee in me, I'm gonna call and have him turned out. With a shadow. That fucker's up to something. I don't know if it has to do with Mrs. St. Juste or not.

—That's it?

—Nope. I also talked to René St. Juste last night. There's a pistol missing from his gun cabinet...a .38 special customized for target shooting.

—Madeline was shot with it?

—Maybe. The coroner tells me the slug was from a .38, but we'd have to have the gun and match ballistics to be sure. By the way, I'm gonna take me a little trip to check out St. Juste's alibi. Want me to pick you up on the way?

—I'm at Wes's.

—Okay. Youall want to drive over to Lafayette with me?

I wondered why I felt such reluctance. —What are you checking?

—René St. Juste says he stayed at the Tidewater Motel Friday night. The clerk at the Tidewater tells the same story.

—Then why would you need to...

—'Cause on the phone that room clerk sounded funny.

—Funny?

—Don't ask, 'cause I can't tell you. But he got my ears to pricking up.

Your ears?

—Gonzo detective, baby. Ears pricking up is almost as serious as nostrils flaring. Or eyes showing white. Besides, after what you told me . . .

So that was it. Maybe I had had to tell Rat what Madeline said, but I didn't have to act as if René were a real suspect. I covered the phone and turned to Wes.

—Rat wants to know if you'd like to drive to Lafayette with him.

—Sure. Is he gonna pick us up?

—Not me. I . . . can't go. I have to see Henry.

—You can see him later.

—No, this morning. I should have gone by last night. There's really nobody else. You know that.

Wes nodded and shrugged. —Tell Rat he knows where I'm at.

The rain was still falling when I reached Henry's immense 1890s gingerbread showplace. The house was well back from St. Charles Avenue and the yard was filled with enormous old oaks and magnolias. The long front porch was low and faced northeast. Rain was blowing up on the painted wood planking. I could see no light through the stained-glass front door, and wondered if he might have gone to stay with someone. But I could think of no one he'd want to be with now.

I rang the doorbell and waited for what seemed a long time. Then, amidst the gloom inside, I thought I saw someone moving. When he opened the door, he looked as if he had aged twenty years overnight. His usually reddish face was pale and unhealthy, his eyes darkly ringed. Thin, iron-gray hair plastered over his forehead, and his robe was soaking wet.

—My God, Uncle Henry, what have you been doing?

He seemed confused by my question.

—Why, I was out back. Where Madeline planted the crepe myrtles. You remember...

I remembered. It was one of Henry's fondest stories about his daughter. Years before I was born, when Madeline had been no more than ten, she'd developed a fascination with those slender trees and their lavender blossoms. She'd gotten money from her father, and she and Lulu had gone shopping the nurseries around town. They'd come back with a carload of small, wretched-looking shrubs and, before anyone could deny the two of them, they'd planted the little trees across one corner of the big backyard. Where they had flourished.

—I hadn't looked at them in years, Henry was saying slowly. —I mean really *looked* at them. I didn't realize how big they'd... He stopped, wiping water from his face. I couldn't tell if it was rain or tears.

I got him out of his robe and sent him upstairs to change into something other than his old-fashioned pajamas, which were cold and wet, too. He'd just as soon be dead now, I thought. His wife is dead, his little girl has gone on before him. The paper doesn't need him. All the bright young men are in charge and doing very well.

When the water was hot, I brewed coffee and waited for him. He looked much better when he came down. He'd shaved and combed his hair. He was wearing that old wine-colored sweater again.

—Coffee, Uncle Henry?

Henry nodded and sipped slowly as he wrestled internally with something for a few moments.

—Tomorrow, he choked out.

—What?

—I'm gonna bury my baby tomorrow.

—But...

—Coroner's office... released her.

—Uncle Henry, that won't leave time for an announcement in the paper. People won't know...

—I don't give a shit, he said in a low voice. —It's not the Comus Ball or the Rex parade. It's a goddamned funeral. It's... Oh, Jesus Christ...

He tried to turn away, but there was no room, no place to turn. He put his head in his hands and sobbed without making a sound. It was somehow much worse than if he had screamed and torn the fabric from the furniture, ripped down the drapes, kicked out the windows, and howled his anguish like a wounded animal to the passersby on St. Charles Avenue.

After what seemed a long time, he raised his head and studied the fire.

—I got to stop this, he said in a strangled voice. —I got to put it behind me. I got to get past it.

He cleared his throat and tried to compose himself. Then he rose and searched the table on the far side of the room. He came back with two glasses of whiskey.

—And I got to go easy on this. I always had a weakness for it. It's like being free out in the woods, fishing in the swamp. You get into liquor, you don't want to come back. Why would you? What's here in this world to call a man back?

—People who love you, I ventured.

—Haw. There's you. I wouldn't give a hoot in hell for the rest of 'em. This is not my town. It's only where I made my living and raised up my little girl. And... Dennie, I've been thinking. With Madeline gone, I want you to be my heir.

—Don't think about that now, Uncle Henry.

—No, I got to think about something. God knows I

got to put my mind on something I care about. Your granddaddy and...your father were my friends. I want to do this. I wanted you to know.

He paused and sipped his liquor. —Something else. I had me a talk with John Maitland. He's going along with you helping him on the case. I want justice, little girl. And you're the only one I trust to give it to me.

I felt a chill rising inside. Henry said justice, but he meant revenge. And for all his love of me, the talk of making me his heir was just a way to...motivate me, to provide for my cooperation. I thought of my own attempt to get Wes's cooperation for Maitland and I realized how Wes must have felt. Intimately.

—Rat's in charge of the investigation. He's good. He'll find whoever did it.

—I know that. But I want to know what Trapp knows. When he knows it. Call Trapp for me. Tell him that. Will you call him now?

I rose to leave. I didn't want to upset Henry more by arguing with him, but I resented his assumption that the district attorney's office and the police department should be instruments of his personal vengeance— when and if a target could be found.

—Rat's in Lafayette right now, and...

—Trapp's in Lafayette? Why would he take up his Sunday to drive over there? And don't tell me it's to check out the gumbo.

—All right. He wanted to speak to the clerk at the motel where René said he spent Friday night.

Henry paused, thinking, rubbing his eyes with the back of his thick red hands.

—Trapp said he didn't think my baby's death was just a B and E felony murder. Now he's checking René's alibi, huh?

—Don't assume anything, Uncle Henry. Just don't..

He stared at me in silence. Then, —No, he said in the softest of voices. —I wouldn't want to do that.

When I reached the house on State Street, I missed Wes and felt almost angry with him, but that was silly. He and Rat had asked me along. I could have driven to Lafayette with them. Why hadn't I?

Then it occurred to me I'd sentenced myself to a long Sunday alone because I feared they might find something in Lafayette, at the Tidewater Motel, that would give substance to Madeline's last fear.

I was trying to imagine René pointing a gun at Madeline, firing it, when I first heard the sound, a quiet scratching of metal against wood, against stone.

A rat, I thought. No matter how much you spend on pest control, no matter how many blocks of poison flavored with peanut butter are scattered in the attic, the pantry, under the house itself, there are always rats.

I took up the poker from beside the fire and walked into the hallway. The sound stopped. It had seemed to be coming from the breakfast room just off the kitchen. A rank of French doors opened into the garden where, in the spring, a paradise of early flowers bloomed. But now the drapes were drawn, and the room was nearly dark.

The sound was coming from behind the drapes. I wanted to run back to the library and pretend I'd heard nothing, but that feeling made me laugh inside. A day or so ago, I'd walked into a half-lit storeroom and faced down a professional killer. Now a mere sound made my flesh creep, goose bumps rise on my arms, the back of my thighs.

I started to draw the drapes, my poker raised, but the sound stopped suddenly and the drapes parted of themselves. One of the doors opened, and a man stepped into the gloomy room.

I took one good swing at him as he sensed my presence and turned toward me. The poker hit his suddenly upraised arm and glanced off. He fell backward against the table.

—No, hey, lady, wait . . .

I drew back to swing again, but then I recognized him. It was Mario, Madeline's chauffeur. He had no weapon, and his hands were thrust out in a gesture of supplication, not of threat.

—Look, I didn't come to . . .

—Breaking and entering, I said, wondering why I was characterizing the crime rather than beating his head in.

—Look, I got to see you, talk to you, that's all.

—No front doors where you come from?

—The cops . . . they got somebody on me. If I tried the front, he'd have picked me up again. Lady, please . . . I'm not gonna hurt you.

—What do you want?

He seemed to draw a deep breath then. His hands were shaking as he held on to the back of a chair.

—I want to make a deal. You got to come with me.

—You're insane.

—No, look . . . that black cop has me made for dropping Mrs. St. Juste, right?

—It's crossed his mind.

—I never did it. I done bad things. But I never hurt anybody.

—So you didn't stop by to confess?

—I'm not even who they think I am.

—What?

—I'm not . . . Mario Truxillo.

I cocked my poker again. Not because he seemed

threatening, but from surprise. He moved back, lifting his hands again.

—Come to my brother's place, will you? Look, I'm a thief. I tell you I'm a thief. But I'm not a killer...

—What's your real name?

—Juan... Juan Truxillo. Mario's my brother. Will you come let me show you?

Later, I'd wonder if I should be committed for doing what I did. Even then, I realized I'd never again be able to give Rat Trapp that certain look of disdain when he talked about Gonzo detective work.

Juan Truxillo was a frightened man. I think that's why I followed when he went out the back way and cut through silent empty backyards to reach his car parked under some trees on Nashville Street. As he opened the door for me, I hesitated one last time, then got in, thinking, You wasted three years in law school. All you really needed was Special Forces training.

We drove down narrow side streets on the river side of St. Charles. Juan Truxillo kept his eyes on the rear-view mirror more than on the street ahead. We crossed over Magazine Street, and finally drew to a stop on a short tree-lined block of Hillary. The rain had started falling again, and it looked closer to eight o'clock than four.

—Look, my brother used to work for a delivery service here in town. There was this accident. He's on workmen's comp now, back in Florida.

—So?

—So when he quit working, I got hold of his chauffeur's license, his references. That's how I got the job with the St. Justes.

—You said you're a thief.

He turned off the ignition and lay back against the car seat.

—Yeah. I been knocking over some places Uptown. For a few months. Nothing rough. Just in and out. You'll see . . .

We walked up to the door of a small weatherbeaten shotgun. As we stepped inside, Juan switched on a flashlight he was carrying and pointed it into the room. It was something to see.

The beam of the light sparkled off a table in the center of the room covered with silver and gold objects. Candlesticks, plates, flatware, boxes, cutlery, hand mirrors, comb and brush sets, piles of studs and cufflinks, money clips, watches, brooches, bracelets, rings, a scattering of what looked to be old coins carefully packaged in plastic envelopes, and, neatly laid out on linen napkins, dozens of sterling snail-holders and matching forks.

Juan handed me the flashlight as he took out a matchbook and began lighting candles in dozens of beautiful candelabras. As the room began to take on a warm, old-fashioned glow, I could see more and more of its contents.

Along one wall, there were shelves hastily, clumsily nailed together. On them were televisions, tape decks, VCRs, every sort of stereo component—including some apparently pulled bodily from automobiles.

Stacked here and there were expensive sets of golf clubs, hunting rifles, shotguns with engraved receivers and polished rare-wood stocks, and fishing equipment —including a large yellow inflatable rubber boat that had the logo of Delta Airlines stenciled on it.

There was much more lying on chairs and piled under the shelves along the walls of the parlor, but my eyes could only take in so much at a time.

—My God . . .

Juan blew out his last match and stared across the table at me, looking like a sullen little boy.

—Look, like I told you . . . I mean I hit some places.

—I see. How many people helped you?

—No . . . nobody. I work hard when I'm working.

—Uh-huh.

—It's a bad habit. Everybody I knew in Miami was hustling. Miami Beach would be cleaned out if it wasn't for the security. But I never hurt nobody. I never hit a place where anybody was home. I was careful about that. I got a little record, but no rough stuff and . . . a terrible childhood, no daddy . . .

—All right. I believe you're a thief. What about it?

—What about it? Look, see this stuff?

He went from one part of the room to another, pointing out items as if at random. Somehow I realized that he knew where everything in the room had come from.

—This is all from a place on Octavia Street. I was cleaning it out that night.

—What night?

Juan looked at me as if I were simpleminded.

—Friday night, when Mrs. St. Juste got dropped. I left before Lulu went home. I never got back till the next morning. When I got done working Octavia, I went over to this bar off Chef Menteur Highway, and this broad and me . . . Tessie Arnault . . . we . . .

I said nothing, still looking at his hoard, amazed that anyone could make off with so much in a few months —and never get caught. Maybe the system was wasting its time. Maybe Crazy Lady was the very best name for the whole silly business, and maybe she should take up knitting straitjackets for herself.

—It's all here, Juan was saying nervously, looking as if he might be wondering whether he'd made the best move in bringing me to his treasure house. —I never moved any of it. Look, if the people come go through it all, they'll have everything back.

—All right.

—So this proves I never hurt Mrs. St. Juste...and look, you could let me plead to a count of simple burglary and talk to the judge and I could go back to Florida and...

—We'll go over to Tulane and Broad and talk about it.

—No way. Look, why you think I got you to come over here? You don't give a shit about theft. You want to hang the guy who offed Mrs. St. Juste, right?

—I'm leaving now. If you want to come with me...

—No, I got to know what you're gonna do for me.

He stepped in front of the door, his expression suddenly hard and frightening. Then he started toward me.

—I'm not gonna do seven to ten for a bunch of junk.

—We'll talk about it.

—Bullshit. I got to know.

He took another step toward me, and I found myself backed up against the table.

—You're getting into assault, Mario, I warned him.

—Juan, he said, and reached out for me.

I already had one hand resting on the table and the other wrapped around a particularly tall single candlestick. I'd been ready to pound a rat an hour before, so I just remembered how I had felt then, and brought the candlestick up and around as hard as I could.

Juan was an accomplished thief, but he wasn't going to make a living as a mugger. He never saw the candlestick coming. It caught him in the side of the head just above his left ear, and he fell backward into a nest of fly rods and nets and tackle boxes as if he'd dropped through the ceiling from the sky. The lighted candles dislodged, flared for a moment on the wooden floor, and went out.

I was wondering if I should hit him again. His eyes were closed, his mouth open, and his head bleeding. I had no idea how hard one hit someone else in the head to keep him out for ten minutes, twenty minutes, an hour. I supposed there was some rule of thumb that every man knew regarding such things, but I didn't know it. Still, Juan looked peaceful enough, and I could see a phone cord snaking through the accumulated loot under a window near the door. Maybe I could have a patrol car here before he woke up. If not, I'd have to give him another twenty minutes—as nearly as I could judge it.

After what seemed a long piece of forever, I found the telephone. I'd already started to dial before I realized it was dead. Dead as in cut off. Of course. What need for phone service? Or the lights? Mario was taking it easy in Florida on workmen's comp, and this was nothing but a warehouse for stolen goods. Any time he wanted, Juan could have fenced the whole contents and been gone in an hour or so. If it hadn't been for Madeline's murder and his cold feet, I was sure that must have been his agenda.

It seemed I was going to have to take a chance on the streets if I wanted to find help. It wasn't the best neighborhood or the worst, but I wasn't likely to get much assistance from the neighbors. They were smart. Once it was dark, they stayed inside.

I walked to the door with my candlestick in hand. Pity the mugger or strong-arm lover who tried to stop me now. It seemed I was into cracking heads. Wes and Rat would never let me hear the end of it.

I reached out to open the door, but it burst open before I could touch it, and I fell backward into a tangled pile of golfing and yachting and trapshooting trophies as two men stepped through the open door. The one in front was carrying a gun.

CHAPTER
8

Have you lost your mind? Wes was saying as he smothered me in his arms. —What the hell are you doing playing detective again?

Rat had tucked away his gun, turned Juan over on his face, and was cuffing him. —Old Mario give you a scare, sweetie?

—No, I lied, proud of the level sound of my voice. —I'm afraid he's going to have a bad headache. But he isn't Mario.

They both stared at me. Rat gave Juan a jerk, flipping him back over. —It's Mario, all right.

—No, that's Juan. Mario is in Florida. They're brothers.

—Horseshit, Rat said. —This is the pachuco I carted down to the pokey. I could pick him out of a barrel of 'em.

—That's right. He's been using his brother's name and I.D. When you let him out, he came to me to make a deal.

Wes was looking around at Juan's stock. He whistled and picked up a shotgun, showed it to Rat.

—It's a Purdy. That thing goes for four grand used. Reckon I could just break it down and . . .

Rat laughed, gave him a nasty look, and took the shotgun from his hands.

—Now everything here belongs to some citizen, brother. I don't want to have to ask you to empty your pockets. Anyhow, you got no business with a shotgun. I don't want to think about you walking around with a shotgun.

—I didn't know there was this much crap in all of Uptown, Wes said, his eyes still on the gun.

—Must not be much left, Rat answered as he jerked Juan to his feet and appeared to throw him out the open door into the night.

—Some tail you had on him, I said.

Rat frowned. —Not a damn thing wrong with the tail. My man had this ding-dong in sight all the way. Didn't you, George?

From out on the porch, an enormous black man in plainclothes looked in. He had to be almost seven feet tall. Juan was tucked under his arm like a package of laundry. He smiled and nodded.

—That was nice what you did, he said to me. —I mean with the candlestick.

—How long will he . . . ?

—Oh about another ten minutes, I judge.

—Thank you.

—Don't mention, Miss Lemoyne.

Wes was grinning as George vanished back into the night. Rat was over at the table quickly sifting through the jewelry piece by piece.

—You can wipe that absurd smile off your face, I told Wes. —I did just fine.

—Yeah, you did. I mean it. You really did.

—Never was a thing to worry about, Rat said distractedly as he looked carefully at a jeweled pendant, shrugged, then put it back with the rest. —George was ready to come through that door like Fist City if things got out of hand. We patched into his radio soon as we got south of Baton Rouge.

—If only somebody could have signaled me, I said, sitting down on a chair full of assorted women's dresses.

—How we gonna do that? If Mario-Juan gets the wind up, we miss this place and he goes back to stir with a zipper on his lip.

He finished with the jewelry and came over to sit next to me. He had to move a pile of cigar boxes out of the way. He looked at the boxes, shook them.

—Lord Jesus, Rat said in awe. —These boxes is full. This is a pile of mint Cubans.

Wes gave him a hard calculating look. —Do I get the Purdy?

Rat thought about it for a moment. —No, he said disgustedly, setting the cigar box down and turning away. —Shit no. Now let's talk about something else.

—Like the jewelry? I asked.

—None of it from the St. Juste house, Rat said. —Right?

—I don't know, I told him. —Madeline had a lot of pieces. I only remember one or two.

—St. Juste had pictures. From what I see here, nothing matches. I'll have ballistics go over the guns, but it seems Mario-Juan was telling the truth.

—Which is more than we can say for St. Juste, Wes said.

I glanced over at Rat. His expression did nothing to set my mind at ease.

—You're back from Lafayette...

—She noticed, Wes said to Rat, looking amused.

—What did you find out? I asked.

Rat took me by the arm and steered me outside. Two uniformed officers stood on the porch.

—Seal it up, Rat told one of them as Wes joined us. —The property folks will be here later.

As we reached his car, Rat glanced at his watch. —I believe we can make the Camellia Grill before the dinner crowd piles in. Want to give it a shot?

Rat looked thoughtful as we drove back toward St. Charles Avenue.

—I had to brace the room clerk at the Tidewater Motel, he said. —But he came along. They all came along. 'Specially when you say "murder" to 'em. He said René paid for the room and had a little deal with the switchboard operator to pick up on his calls and forward 'em over here to the city...

—Well...

—But the clerk never saw him on a Friday night. Not rarely or once in a while. Not ever.

Wes laughed. —So Gonzo Dick squeezed till he got a phone number out of Prelieux.

—Prelieux?

—This Cajun clerk, Rat went on. —Since it wasn't our jurisdiction, and since René does a lot of work out of Lafayette, I thought well, I better lay bucks on this ass instead of twist his nose off. No need to get the authorities stirred up over there. Next thing we know, they'd tip St. Juste.

—The police? I asked, surprised.

—He didn't kill anybody in Lafayette, Wes observed. —And René's an old coonass from those parts, too.

—One never knows, do one? Rat observed. —Maybe they'd cooperate, maybe not. Why try 'em? We laid a bill on Prelieux, and he gave us a phone number. We run it by the New Orleans CrissCross Directory, and it turned out to be a nice snug little place down in the Quarter.

I realized what that had to mean. Madeline had been right—at least about René's having other feminine interests. It wasn't surprising. South Louisiana had never been part of anyone's Puritan culture. Every woman suspects her husband might be amusing himself in bedrooms other than her own—and many women, if not most, are right.

—So René has a lady friend, I said finally.

—Nobody said that . . . yet, Rat said quietly. —Hell, maybe he likes little boys. You know how that old country blood goes when it starts breaking down.

—I think you can put that notion out of mind, I said dryly. —René St. Juste is . . . I wonder who she can be?

—I'm gonna need me a search warrant, Rat reflected as he pulled into a parking place on South Carrollton. —Maybe he's got her picture and letters and all manner of crap in that little place in St. Ann Street.

We got out and started walking toward the Camellia Grill. The night air chilled me. Wes noticed and pulled me close to him.

—Sorry about your old friend René, he said.

—Wes, he's not on his way to the electric chair.

Rat nodded. —That's right, honey. He's not. I still want to see inside that little love nest of his. I surely do. And I'd like to do it tonight. Before René-baby knows.

We paused in front of the Camellia Grill. The best hamburgers, the best omelettes in New Orleans or maybe anywhere. The front looks like an old plantation house cut down to cartoon scale. Inside, people sat at the long curved counters. Black chefs in immaculate whites moved from station to station with bewildering speed. I saw an omelette fly into the air and fall back again onto a gleaming grill.

—It's Sunday, I said.

—Uh, yes, Rat came back, his face revealing nothing.

—You think it has to be tonight?

—What I think is, Prelieux over in Lafayette could be on the phone to old René any time now. And a call from Prelieux would set St. Juste off like a bottle rocket.

Inside, the grill was warm and the odor of cooking meat and eggs and French fries seemed to enfold us. We were hardly seated before a counterman had taken our order and moved on.

—No omelette tonight? Wes asked.

—Two hamburgers and fries, I told him. —I may not hold the onions, either. It's been an awfully macho evening.

We sat eating in silence. We were tired, and I wished there were some way for me to avoid the next step. But I couldn't. It was my step to take, and we all knew it.

—I could go by a judge's home. Elena Quintero lives Uptown.

—Maybe you ought to pick a lighter judge, Wes said through a mouthful of French fries. —They say that broad will find you in contempt for hard breathing.

—Only over the phone, I told him. —She's tough all right. But I think you guys may have enough to make probable cause.

Rat pursed his lips. —If she wants to, she can believe that. If she don't want to . . .

—Why wouldn't she want to? I asked him.

—Baby, everybody Uptown knows everybody else. Now why is she gonna go shaking up the natives 'cause René St. Juste has got a little *maison de rendezvous* in the Quarter?

—She's not Uptown. She just lives Uptown. Elena Quintero's people were Cuban immigrants, and she grew up in the Latin Channel. She still lives riverside of Magazine Street. Besides, René lied about being in Lafayette the night Madeline was killed. That's enough for anybody to keep checking.

Rat shrugged. —Okay... Let's see what the lady judge has up her robe... I mean, her sleeve.

We drove down St. Charles to Felicity and turned toward the Mississippi River. Rat followed my directions until we were parked out in front of the Quintero house in the lower Garden District.

—Not that much of a house, Wes said, looking at the 1920s wooden shotgun. —You'd think a judge could do better for herself.

—She was elected by the Latin immigrants who settled in these old houses. Politicians don't move away from their power base. Didn't you know?

I mounted the wooden steps to the porch and stood shivering after I pressed the bell. The rain had started in once more.

A woman dressed in white answered the door, and I asked for Judge Quintero. For a moment, I thought she was a maid. Then I realized she was wearing a nurse's uniform.

—Wait in here. I'll see if Señora Quintero is available, she said, and vanished behind a door of dark wood.

The living-room floor was varnished red pine planks, and the walls were plaster, painted an off-white. The furnishings were Spanish Provincial, crudely carved but tasteful Mexican tables and chairs. Heavy oak cases full of books filled the walls between tall windows. Outside in back a garden of verdant tropical plants was dimly visible by the light of a large wrought-iron gas lantern. As I watched the rain fall through the gaslight, I wondered if Elena had been ill. Against one wall an oxygen tank was propped beside a folded wheelchair.

Elena walked into the room quickly, looking well though tired, obviously surprised to see me.

—Denise ... What a nice surprise.

—There's some business ... but I feel I'm intruding, Judge.

—Try Elena. I leave the title back with the robe at Tulane and Broad. But not my duties. What is it?

—If someone's ill ...

She pushed a dark lock of hair back from her forehead with an exhausted gesture and sat down, pointing me into a chair opposite.

—It's my husband, Paul.

—I'm sorry. I hope he'll be better soon.

Elena's smile was polite, but there was no warmth or humor in it.

—Thank you. But he won't be. Soon now, he won't be anything at all.

—I can see you tomorrow at court, I said, wishing I hadn't come to take moments from her and her husband.

—No, she said wearily. —If you came, you have a reason. Tell me.

I did. Of course she'd heard about Madeline's death. It seemed she'd even heard that the police had taken someone into custody. But when I mentioned René and gave her our grounds for a search warrant, she seemed shocked.

—Surely René St. Juste's not a suspect?

—He's ... under investigation. He lied to Captain Trapp as to his whereabouts on the night of his wife's death—and it seems he has this little place in the Quarter.

I wasn't sure she was listening. She seemed distracted, head down, eyes moving quickly back and
forth as if she were reading in the pattern of the woven
rug some invisible document only she had eyes to see.

—No, she said at last, a little more loudly than she
needed to. —No, I can't issue you a warrant.

—I beg your pardon?

—I don't see probable cause, Denise. Obviously, the
man wants to keep his personal indiscretions private.
That doesn't constitute evidence of murder.

—No, but it could be a motive. Madeline was a
wealthy woman, and there's reason to believe René's
having financial difficulties . . .

Elena raised her eyes and gave me a piercing look.

—You were close to Madeline St. Juste . . . and her
father.

—That's so.

—Is this . . . a family vendetta? Is Henry Holman determined to lay Madeline's death at the feet of her husband?

I stared back at her for a long moment.

—I work for the district attorney, Judge Quintero, I
told her, —not Henry Holman. Besides, he's too
brokenhearted to be looking for scapegoats. I'm here
because Captain Trapp and I think a search of that
apartment on St. Ann is necessary to the investigation.

—I'm sorry, she said. —I can't help you tonight. Perhaps tomorrow . . .

—Don't give it a moment's thought, I said as I got to
my feet. —By this time tomorrow, I'll have seen the
inside of that apartment.

—I'd advise you . . .

I smiled. —I didn't come for advice, Judge. I came for
a warrant.

I found my own way out, angry that I'd been wrong

about Elena Quintero. When I climbed into the car and slammed the door, Rat glanced across Wes.

—Ah...

—Ah what? I snapped.

—Ah ha. No go.

—That's right. Drive.

—You got another judge in mind?

—No. It's Sunday night and without good probable cause... Damn judges, and this system, too.

Rat faked looking shocked. He nodded toward Wes.

—Not in front of the child, Dennie.

Wes made an idiot face, and I couldn't help laughing.

—My place, Wes said. —When things go wrong, I like to drink.

—What do you do when things go right? Rat grinned.

—Well...

Rat sat on Wes's sofa sipping what Wes liked to call a martini. I was drinking the white wine he kept in the refrigerator for me.

—Come morning, I'm gonna drag old St. Juste in for questioning.

—Funeral's in the morning, Wes said.

—Just after, Rat said, his voice harsh, cruel. —Like I mean *just* after. I'm gonna pick that sonofabitch up at the cemetery.

—But Rat... everyone will be there, I said.

—Uh-huh. God and all the nice Uptown folks. Price of lying to a cop, sugar. Nothing says I got to tiptoe up to his goddamn fucking St. Charles mansion in the dead of night to snag him for questioning.

Wes shook his head while he shook more martinis.

—You do play rough, old sport.

Somehow, coming from Wes, that irked Rat.

—Listen, gizmo, when you lie to a cop, that makes you an honorary nigger—and you *know* how we handle niggers.

Wes poured two ice-cold martinis, and I decided to sample Wes's. It wasn't bad. Perhaps I was just too tired to be critical. I wanted to argue with Rat about René, but I didn't have the heart—or was it the energy?

—You think René'll come across? Wes asked.

Rat shrugged and turned to me. —I got to tell you, I don't give a shit if he comes across or not. If he cooperates, we'll check out that St. Ann apartment and talk to his lady-friend before nightfall. If he don't, I'm gonna charge his ass and send what we got over to Denise's office.

—Rat, you can't get an indictment on what you have, I told him.

—I know. But then we got René-baby in the hot box while I go on looking, don't we?

Wes shook his head in mock—or was it real?—admiration.

—Now that's Gonzo, he laughed as Rat and I sipped our drinks.

CHAPTER
9

The next morning I took a hat with a small veil and a black dress from my closet. It was the fourth time I had worn the same thing to a funeral, but I refused to buy another. Let this one dress carry all the grief, the loss, the burden of tears shed and yet to be shed.

Wes came by, and we drank coffee together in the library. Outside, the rain was falling again, a cold sleet-laced rain that seemed just right for a funereal morning.

—Do you think he's going to do it? I asked Wes.

—Who do what?

—Rat. Arrest René at the cemetery.

Wes gave me a puzzled look, as if he could hardly believe I was asking the question.

—If you don't want to see it, I'll bring you home from the cathedral.

—It seems . . . so uncalled for.

He frowned. I should have known better than to

mention it. The two of them take up for each other no matter how outrageous the circumstances. Men in groups. Theirs is a group of two. I love them both, but I hate the way their closeness keeps everyone else—including me—at a distance.

—It's called for. That bastard St. Juste looked Rat right between the eyes and lied like a sonofabitch. You want the word going out that you can josh the cops and still get the kid-glove bit? Anyhow, you should be glad. St. Juste offed that lady you loved so much.

—That's absurd. There's not even the beginning of enough evidence to convict. If we went to trial tomorrow, he'd walk.

He stared at me in disgust.

—Only if St. Juste could get a couple of these Uptown zombies on his jury. Maybe they'd let murder pass. Herd together. Act like it never happened.

—You've already tried and convicted him, haven't you? God, you make me angry, I almost shouted at him. —You don't know what justice means.

I walked out of the room and found my coat and an umbrella. The foyer was freezing, and there came over me a sudden feeling of loss that had nothing at all to do with Madeline. I was wondering if Wes and I could ever be happy, really happy. Together.

The flagstoned area in front of St. Louis Cathedral was filled with people in black and muted colors, umbrellas overhead. They stood huddled in clumps watching as Madeline's casket was carried into the space before Jackson Square from a hearse parked on St. Ann Street. The pallbearers seemed as aged and gray as the morning. Only Hugh D'Anton was less than sixty. The others bowed under the weight of the deaths they carried. The rain had slackened for a little while, but people's breaths were misting in the cold November morning. When the coffin had passed, all of us straggled into line and entered the cathedral.

As we looked for a place in the pews, someone came up to us. I think it was Jerry Waggaman, a boy I had gone to school with at Tulane Law.

—Denise, he said somberly, —Mr. Holman wants you with him.

—I'm with Mr. Colvin, I told him without thinking.

He studied Wes for a moment as if he recognized the name.

—I'm sure that will be fine, he answered, and gestured for us both to follow him.

Henry sat in the front pew, arms folded, eyes almost closed. His face was gray, like that of the old men, his friends, who had carried his daughter into the church. He didn't look up when we sat down in the pew a little distance from him. Then I saw René coming up the other aisle. He paused on Henry's side at the pew we were all sitting in. For a moment, Henry made no sign. Then he looked up at René. I couldn't see Henry's face, but René's grew more pale than it had been before. Finally, Henry slid down the pew toward us. He moved much farther down than he needed to simply to provide space for René. So that he and René each sat isolated, alone, staring forward as the priest and the acolytes entered to begin Madeline's last ceremonial.

I remember almost nothing of the requiem mass that followed. Nor can I remember what was passing through my mind as I rose when I was supposed to rise, knelt when everyone else knelt—except for Henry, who was no Catholic, who neither rose nor knelt but simply kept his arms folded and his eyes fastened on the flower-covered casket that seemed so out of place in the austere surroundings of the cathedral on a raw, dark day.

Then we were at St. Louis Cemetery. Wes and I stood to one side of the Holman mausoleum as the priest blessed stones and ashes that had been blessed a hundred times before. The rain started up again, and people who had paid their respects began drifting away, trying to get to their cars before the downpour that seemed likely began to come down.

—You want to see it through to the end? Wes asked me. His hair was wet with rain because he was too tall to fit under the umbrella with me comfortably, and anyhow he disliked umbrellas.

—I don't know, I said. —I suppose so. Madeline would never have left me till... She stayed behind when we buried Grandpère. After my father left with all his assistants, she insisted I go home with her... for a drink, she said, or as many drinks as I needed. Anyhow, I have to see Uncle Henry.

—That's fine, Wes said. —I just thought you might not want to be here when...

I glanced around then. The casket was set on a catafalque in front of the open door of the tomb. The priest had knocked at the door with his censer, and the door had come open. A few yards away, pointedly distanced from one another, Henry and René stood watching. René wore an expensive raincoat and held a matching umbrella over his head. Henry stood in a brown suit with unfashionably wide lapels. His head was bare, and he had no umbrella. A few yards behind the two of them, I saw Rat Trapp. He wore a black leather trenchcoat he'd bought in Germany years ago. A uniformed policeman beside him held an umbrella over his head.

His expression told me nothing as I watched his eyes moving across the diminishing circle of people as if he were looking for someone he knew—or someone he knew something about.

—Wes . . . I started.

—It's going down the minute the priest slams that door, baby.

—Would you mind if I went to Henry now? He's soaked through, and . . .

Wes kissed me on the cheek. His lips were cool. —You go ahead. I want to talk to Rat. You going to the office after this?

—God yes. I couldn't stand to be at home alone.

—Maybe you'll go by Holman's place with him for a little while.

I nodded. —Maybe so. I'll see what he wants, what he needs.

He kissed me again and moved away. When I made my way through the few people who still remained and held my umbrella over Henry, I thought he hadn't even noticed.

—They're gonna close her up in there, he said. —She won't ever see the spring again. She won't see anything.

—Uncle Henry . . . I started to say.

—I'm never gonna let this drop, you know. I've got money enough to reach the sonofabitch if I have to send men to the moon.

—Who? Who would you send them after? I asked.

He almost turned toward René, but then the pallbearers were lifting the casket and carrying it into the tomb. I saw Henry's lips trembling.

—If it takes all the days of my life and the last goddamned dime I've got . . . he whispered hoarsely.

The last blessing was given and such final words as

there are were spoken. I took Henry's arm and tried to point him toward the limousine that had brought him to the cemetery. I had gotten him under way, the cold rain coming from the northwest, blowing under the umbrella and punishing our faces, when I heard Rat's voice to my left and behind us.

—Mr. St. Juste ...

—Yes ... ?

—I'd like you to come over to Tulane and Broad with me for a little while.

—Am I ... under arrest?

—I didn't say that. There are ... I have some problems with your statement.

—Then I don't have to come?

—Oh yes, sir, you do. It's not whether you're gonna come. It's how. For a talk or for a stay. It's all the same to me.

Even as I prayed Henry had not heard, I felt his arm pull away from me. He turned and stared across at René and Rat and the uniformed officer.

—You taking him in, Captain?

Rat looked at Henry without answering. Then he turned his attention back to René as people, under their umbrellas, on their way out, stopped, watched, and whispered to one another.

—Well, Mr. St. Juste, how's it gonna be? We don't want to stand around here in the rain and catch pneumonia, do we?

—No, René said, his resistance melting.

I watched as Rat led him down the wet brick-paved way between the dark mausoleums. René's shoulders slumped. He looked almost as old as Henry, as broken, as disconsolate. Under a tree a little distance apart, Wes stood watching, his eyes following the three as if he were composing a photograph, something devoted to death and remembrance. I knew he was composing something else: another entry in his brief against New Orleans. Then he looked back at Henry and me for a moment before he strode down the path that led to the exit and vanished in the smoky rain.

Henry and I rode back to his house in the limo. It felt good to be warm, and there was a bar inside. Henry poured us each a stiff glass of bourbon, but his mind was somewhere else. Enjoying vengeance before the fact, I suspected. I wondered if he'd settled on René after the scene in St. Louis Cemetery.

—I didn't know you'd bought a limo and hired a chauffeur, I said.

Henry threw down his drink and stared forward as if he were intent on the rain slapping the windshield.

—I didn't, he said at last. —This belongs to the funeral parlor. Even the whiskey's theirs. It's supposed to help going to and from the graveyard. It don't.

—No, I answered. —Nothing helps. Except time.

He looked across at me almost furtively—as if he feared saying too much. —Oh yeah, they say that helps. They're goddamn liars, and I got no time, anyhow.

—You can't bring her back, Uncle Henry.

—I can send somebody after her, he answered. —I sure as hell can do that. Then he fell silent as if he had said aloud the one thing he least wanted me to hear.

—You saw what you saw, and now you're fixed on René. That's it, isn't it?

—I never liked the sonofabitch. What kind of man wears jewelry? Gold rings, bracelet of solid gold links —that gold pendant around his neck heavy enough to tie down a hog. Hell, Dennie, the bastard always looked like a damned pimp even with his English tweeds...

—English tweeds...?

—He even made those look cheap. He never loved Madeline a day in his life. He wanted money and place, come out of the swamps to get 'em any way he could... and now...

—I think they loved each other.

—Oh, she loved him all right. And he loved her... to death.

After I saw Henry into the house with a promise that he'd change his wet clothes before he went down to the paper, I had the limo driver drop me at Tulane and Broad. The rain had paused once more, and I thought to check in with Rat before I went to my office.

In front of Central Lockup, I stopped and bought a copy of the *Item* out of a machine. The next installment of "The Hit Parade" stared back at me. It detailed the execution of a Honduran drug dealer outside a small café down in the ninth ward. He'd been strangled behind the wheel of his car, and the car driven into a nearby warehouse and covered with old packing crates. It had been months before he was found, and only then because the stench had become so terrible that workers refused to carry shipments in and out of the building. They thought a big rat had died, Wes's confidential informant said, and they were right.

I dropped the paper in a waste can and caught the elevator to Rat's office. When I got there, the door was closed.

Wes was sitting on the desk Rat's former assistant, Maxine Hawkins, had used. He had his own copy of the *Item* in hand, reading the sports section.

—They've been in there almost an hour. Not a sound. How's the old man?

—Grim. Rat's little morality play convinced him René killed Madeline. He's already planning how to even the score.

Wes shrugged. —You want to play the cops, you got to pay the cops. What do you say we talk about something else? I don't give a shit about Renny-baby.

—Why do youall hate him so much? You, Rat, Henry...

—You didn't hear? He kills women. For money.

I was going to come back at him point for point, to show that no one was even beginning to make a case against René, but as I opened my mouth Rat's door opened. He stepped out and looked from me to Wes, one of his long slender Marsh-Wheeling cigars clenched between his teeth.

—You I can't use, he told Wes. —Gimme a call when your stomach growls. After eight.

Then he looked back at me. —Counselor, you I need in here. If you got nothing pressing.

I nodded and started into the office, leaving Wes to argue with Rat. I knew what the argument was going to be about, and it reminded me that I needed to get some things clear with Wes myself. He was going to have to draw a line in his head between what he heard officially and what he heard privately. I wasn't going to see Madeline's death as the foundation for another series. He'd probably call it "Lady Killer," and I was having enough trouble with Maitland because of "The Hit Parade."

René stood at Rat's big window looking out at the leaden sky. His hair was still wet with rain, and he looked much older than he had a few days before.

René had always managed to keep a fine deep tan, but now his face was mottled, as if the tan had come from chemicals rather than nature. As I moved closer to him, I could smell alcohol. When he turned and saw me, his eyes quickly slid away.

—Hello, Dennie. Are you here on business?

—It seems so, I said. —Maitland put me on Madeline's ... death.

—I thought it was like doctors, he said abstractedly. —I thought they didn't let you work on ... family.

—Henry asked, I told him. —Maitland understood.

René nodded and lit a cigarette. His hands were shaking. He held the match too long and it dropped from his fingers. He stared at it on the floor for a moment before he picked it up, as if he could not relate his burned fingers to that bit of charred paper on the carpet.

—I wish ... it were someone else, he said slowly.

—I wish it were no one.

Rat came in and watched the two of us for a few moments. Then he sat down behind his desk, keeping his eyes on René all the time.

—I expect we might want to fill in Miss Lemoyne on where we are, Mr. St. Juste.

René nodded absently, put out the cigarette that he had hardly touched in an ashtray on Rat's desk. His eyes still on René, Rat leaned forward and flicked a long piece of ash off his cigar into the tray. It almost covered René's cigarette butt. I was beginning to understand what "Gonzo" meant. Then Rat spoke to me, his eyes still on René, his voice low, mirthless, accusatory.

—It seems Mr. St. Juste here admits he's been leading what you Uptown folks call a double life, Counselor. You know, the little arrangement he had going with the hotel clerk in Lafayette, the quiet tasteful place he keeps in St. Ann Street.

As Rat spoke, René looked down at his hands as they twisted uncontrollably in his lap. Under other circumstances, he might have seemed like a truant being lectured or a salesman about to be sacked by his boss. He looked hopeless, humiliated—beyond even the appearance of offering a defense.

—Mr. St. Juste allows as how he and Mrs. St. Juste had been drifting apart for a long time.

I said nothing.

—And he tells me he's been meeting some lady at that nice little place of his on St. Ann almost every Friday evening.

—She'll testify René was with her the night Madeline was . . . ?

Rat cut me off. —No, Counselor, seems that's too easy for Mr. St. Juste.

—I don't understand.

René looked up at me, shamefaced. —I can't tell the captain the lady's name, Dennie. She's . . . in a position to be hurt, very badly hurt.

—As badly as Madeline was hurt?

René looked away.

—Seems Mrs. St. Juste was on to Mr. St. Juste's goofing around, Rat continued.

I stared at René for a long moment. He nodded without meeting my eyes.

—I told . . . the lady that Madeline knew about us. She said she was sorry. We all have enough pain to bear without adding to it. She wasn't going to be part of causing Madeline any more heartache. She left the apartment early.

—So you see Mr. St. Juste is in what we call on the streets deep shit. He won't give us the lady's name, and, even if he did, she couldn't say where he was when Mrs. St. Juste died.

—I was there, in the apartment, René flared, show-ing the first touch of spirit since I'd come into the room. —When . . . when the lady left, I tried to work. I drank my way through a quart of whiskey. I remem-ber crying.

Rat stood and walked around the desk. He sat down on its edge and lowered his head until it was only inches from René's.

—A man might go to drinking and crying if his lady love had took off on him. Or he might go home and pick up a quarrel with his wife where he'd left it earlier. Then if something awful happened and he found him-self back at his little apartment wondering why he'd done what he done . . . a man might even drink and cry over that.

—No, René almost shouted. —It wasn't like that. I didn't hurt her.

—But you fought with her? Or had you already done too much drinking to know what you did? Maybe you don't even remember.

—No, none of that's true. I stayed at the apartment till I came home the next day and found all of you there.

—You argued with Mrs. St. Juste real bad Friday morning.

—No . . .

—Yes. Don't say no, 'cause I've got a statement. If you say no, you're gonna be walking right into a brick wall. Like with that Lafayette motel bullshit story of yours.

—Statement, I said. —What statement?

Rat smiled humorlessly. —I talked to the house-keeper, Lulu Washington. She heard stuff.

—Yes?

—She remembers they argued a lot.

René tried to shrug, but it seemed his shoulders weren't functioning properly. There was a desperate look in his eyes that I'd never seen before. I wouldn't have guessed that anything could have shaken his self-confidence so deeply.

—Married people . . . argue, he said, his voice trailing away.

—Sure they do, Rat answered, his eyes never leaving René's. —Some of 'em get married for that. But the morning you left for your usual Friday in Lafayette, Lulu says it got real bad. She couldn't help overhearing all the way in the kitchen because you people were yelling.

René nodded. —Madeline had suspected something for months, and she couldn't leave it alone. She wanted to know who I was seeing. Friday morning, she told me she'd found out.

—And she wasn't bluffing? I put in. —She named her?

René took a deep breath and nodded silently. He simply wasn't going to identify the woman. Perhaps he thought protecting her was all that he could salvage from this vicious mess, and he was determined to do that.

—Then Madeline said she'd make sure everyone knew. That we'd never draw a serene, peaceful breath in New Orleans. She meant it. I know she did.

—Right, Rat snapped. —Question is, just how far would you go to keep that from happening?

He stepped back around his desk and opened a drawer. He took out the small leather-bound book had seen on Madeline's secretary desk the day of her death. He held Madeline's diary in his hand, riffling through the pages. Then he read in a low steady voice.

"... like living alone. No, much worse than that because one realizes the terms of living alone. This thing that has come upon René has changed him, changed him utterly. This morning, the quarrel broke out again. We both said terrible things. At last, as he left, he stared at me as if he didn't know me—no, as if he wished I were dead. I think he does, and when I remember what sort of man he was years ago when we met, I know that he could translate that wish into action. Perhaps I wouldn't mind. Perhaps it would be better for us both. . . ."

René looked startled, horrified, as Rat set down the diary and let its cover fall closed. Rat shook his head and brought the tips of his fingers together.

—I tell you what, Mr. St. Juste. We've been talking, as you might say, informally. But this thing's like an iceberg. Little on top, lots more down below. I believe you ought to call yourself an attorney while I go hustle up a warrant for that little place in St. Ann Street.

René stood up, leaned forward across the desk.
—Am I under arrest, Captain?

Rat studied him as he rolled his cigar around in his mouth.

—No, sir. But you're on notice that you're the target of a criminal investigation. Don't attempt to leave the city or to remove objects from the place on St. Charles or the apartment on St. Ann. Don't attempt to withdraw more than one thousand dollars from any bank account, personal or joint. Don't write checks on any account for anything except ongoing or ordinary obligations and expenses.

I had no idea where Rat was getting this string of

prohibitions that he recited like a Miranda warning. It had no precedent in Louisiana law. Then it struck me. Gonzo was working again. Rat had no power whatever to enforce anything he was saying—but it was obvious that René supposed he did, and the sudden brutal realization of constraints was working on him as well as a pair of handcuffs might have.

—You don't need a warrant. I'll...take you there, René almost whispered.

—Ah, Rat said, and paused. —See, I think a good lawyer would be the best thing now, Mr. St. Juste. When I bust you, I want it to be righteous. I don't want some judge to start in whining that I didn't dot an "i" or cross a "t." You understand that, don't you?

René slammed his fist into the desk. Papers jumped, and even Rat seemed surprised.

—I didn't kill my wife, René shouted hoarsely. —I didn't do it. In Christ's name...Why would I need a lawyer if I'm innocent?

Rat shrugged and turned to me. —What do you say, Counselor? Reckon we can take up Mr. St. Juste's invitation to St. Ann Street without prejudicing our case?

—I think so, I said quietly, resenting Rat's using me as the good-guy cop in his down and dirty head wars. He knew he had me cornered, and he wanted to see which abstraction I was going to serve when we reached the choke point. For all I knew, he'd make a detailed report to Wes when they met for a late supper afterward.

—Well, let me get a little housekeeping done around here, and we'll go see your little spot on St. Ann, Rat said.

Then he stepped out of the office, letting the door close softly behind him, still playing me as much as René. I turned to look at René, but he was trying to light a cigarette, his eyes on the match, his hands shaking. Finally he drew a deep breath and let his eyes rise to meet mine.

—What happened, René? How did it come to... this?

René shrugged. —How can I say? I'm inside it, Dennie. Madeline... changed. When she realized we'd never have a child, something changed in her. She drew away from me as if it were my fault. She knew better—doctors at Ochsner Clinic told her so. But it didn't matter. It was as if I had been... withholding something from her. Then her mother died.

—I know. It hurt her very much.

René shrugged. —Maybe it did, maybe it didn't. I don't know. By then, it was so bad between us we weren't sharing our thoughts. But whatever she felt, it was an excuse to stay in bed half the day, to turn down any invitation we might get. She stopped putting on makeup. When people stopped by, she'd stay in her room.

He lit another cigarette, easily this time, and blew a stream of smoke at the window.

—I don't know, Denise. Maybe she did it to me, or I did it to her. Maybe we did it to one another. Maybe marriages get old and molder and fall apart, but the people go on with them like wearing shabby clothes. Who wants to try it again, all over again? Maybe if there'd been a child... Who knows?

He was silent for a moment and it occurred to me how little young people understand the adults with whom they've grown up. They aren't people at all. They're monuments, locations in our own intense, trivial, burgeoning lives. A few years ago no one could have convinced me that René and Madeline had anything but the best of marriages—the very kind of happy, carefree marriage I wanted for myself. But then aren't we as divided from one another by age, by generation, as by sex or race or nationality? Still, I should have known. Perhaps I *had* known and somehow pushed the knowledge aside.

Had I ignored Madeline's cry for help at our luncheon because I unconsciously took René's side, understood his need for a younger woman, even imagined that that woman might have, under the right circumstances, been me? I think I blushed at that thought. At least, I should have.

It was a relief when Rat returned, ending the private moment alone with René, announcing a squad car was ready to take us to St. Ann Street.

CHAPTER
10

The trip down to the Quarter only took a few minutes. René opened the outside door of a red brick building near the corner of Chartres Street.

Once, long ago, the place had been a luxurious private home with ceilings twelve or thirteen feet high. What had been a long entrance hall opening into parlors and a dining room and library was now the lobby of a very nice apartment complex. At the back of the lobby, double French doors looked out on a deep courtyard where the sun must have scarcely ever reached.

We wound our way up a wide curved stairway to a second-story apartment that had been reconstructed out of several of the old bedrooms. Floor-to-ceiling windows on two sides offered a dramatic view of Jackson Square. The walls were a smooth plastered off-white, going toward gray, the floors a dark parquet with alternating blocks of wood that looked like mahogany and ebony. There were loosely woven drapes shot through with a subdued pattern of black-and-silver thread, and the whole design of the place seemed poised between cool eastern Mediterranean white and Italian black and silver. The furniture was an eclectic blend of pieces from half a dozen countries and as many periods. The place was breathtaking in its richness and simplicity.

—It's lovely, I said to René as I walked to one of the windows and looked out toward the square. —Somehow I expected...

—A small efficiency at the far end of Bourbon? With broken plaster and peeling wallpaper? Hot soiled sheets?

—And a balcony with broken boards and an old battered aluminum shade up above, I finished.

René nodded. —There were moments when I would have settled for that. Just to be free of whatever had taken over Madeline.

As we spoke, I could sense Rat moving around the apartment behind us—digging and delving, as Wes liked to say.

—Ah, Rat was saying softly as he examined papers and something like a mailing tube lying on the lowered shelf of a beautiful old secretary desk. He was shaking the cylindrical paper tube. Then he set it down and turned toward René.

—This is your desk, Mr. St. Juste? he asked in the most polite of tones.

—Yes. Of course. I do a lot of work here. You can see...

—And this map tube...? Rat interrupted.

—Surveys of offshore areas for lease in the Dunbar Block. I've been...

Rat motioned me over, took my arm, and pulled me next to him—as if somehow it was important for the two of us to be side by side as the next question was asked.

—I shook out your maps, Mr. St. Juste.

—All right.

—And see what come with them?

The three of us looked down at the desktop. There, among scattered papers, lay a small gold-and-diamond earring designed in the shape of a scallop-shell. It wasn't the kind of jewelry one sees every day, but I recognized it. I had seen it often before. The last time I had seen it had been at the Caribbean Room in the Pontchartrain Hotel.

—Can you identify that piece, Mr. St. Juste? Rat asked in a soothing neutral tone, revealing more by his voice than if he had drawn his gun.

I looked up at René to see if he would acknowledge what I already knew for certain. His face was drained of blood, his eyes fixed on the earring as if it were some sort of lethal device. His cigarette had fallen from his hand and was smoldering on the desktop among his papers.

—I've cooperated enough, Captain, he said in a small constricted voice. —I want a lawyer present before I . . .

—That's fine, Mr. St. Juste, Rat said in the same flat inexpressive voice, no louder than he had spoken before. —I thought as how that little piece belonged to your wife. It was stolen the night she was murdered. I suppose you don't have an idea how it got here? No? Well, you have the right to remain silent. If you do not exercise the right, anything you say can and will be used against you. . . .

• • •

At ten the next morning, I was in the criminal justice building walking down the long high-ceilinged corridor toward Elena Quintero's courtroom. From half a block away, I saw him sprawled on a bench reading one of those miserable paranoid suspense novels in which everyone betrays everyone else, and the only person you really suppose to be decent is worse than the villains, and the military and the corporations and the churches are all plotting to take over and make robots out of us.

Wes looked up and smiled. —This one is really good. The captured and tortured hero gets hold of a fifty caliber machine gun, and he gets the drop on a platoon of teenage KGB recruits, and he . . .

—I know.

—You haven't read this. I only bought it day before yesterday.

—I don't have to read it. I know what youall do when you get hold of machine guns.

We exchanged a long look, and Wes said nothing. I sat down beside him.

—You're in on the bail hearing for Bluebeard? Wes asked.

—Maitland wants me on the case. And the name's St. Juste.

—You could have squealed personal relationship. He'd have to let you off. If I were him, I wouldn't have you within a mile of this mess.

—A case is a case. If it's not blood kin. Or someone with whom you're doing business.

—I thought you were up to your gorgeous thighs in doubt about this thing.

—I am.

—So you're gonna help prosecute. Oh boy . . . Too

bad Louisiana got rid of the portable electric chair. They could plug it in a wall socket and sauté that coonass wife-killing bastard in the bedroom where they found her.

I had never noticed before how cynical his smile could be.

—Well, you didn't invent the system, Wes said. —But you've got more headaches coming.

—Don't tell me. I don't want to know.

—Santo's not the only one Marvell's gonna try to spring. How do you like him representing St. Juste?

I stared at him for a moment. In my very worst legal nightmares, I'm always at the prosecutor's table alone, and Jock Marvell is defending. And I lose and I lose and I lose.

—You're not kidding, are you?

—Not even a little. He just signed on as attorney of record a while ago. Priss Wyman, Quintero's secretary, is an old friend. She told me. Fireworks, baby. Rockets, Roman candles, prosecutors self-immolating... Then he turned serious. —You ought to shake loose of this one, Dennie. You don't need it. If it tries, let Maitland walk in there and have Marvell jam his foot up his butt. I could enjoy that.

—So could I, I admitted. —But I have to stay with it. It's feeling funny, and René is entitled to...

—Ten feet of rope, six feet of dirt. In an unfashionable part of St. Louis Cemetery.

I didn't answer. All the men I cared for seemed to be reliving the nineteenth century in their fantasies. There was nothing for it but to keep on keeping on with what I was supposed to be doing and hope we could avoid really ugly encounters with one another. Wes was disgusted with my attitude about René. I knew Rat felt the same, and I didn't even want to think about what

Henry would say when he heard who René had defending him.

Judge Quintero had just taken the bench when we walked in. I left Wes outside the bar and joined Maitland at the State's table. John had his eye on René... no, actually on Jock Marvell. Maitland didn't give a damn who the defendant was, but he'd simply love to break Marvell's winning streak against the office. I didn't blame him. It was demoralizing the troops. Lawyers are a little like racehorses. Winning improves them. Losing breaks them down. The staff of the Orleans Parish D.A.'s office had been saddle-broken and rubbed sore by Marvell. For years. Maitland wanted this case to try, whether there *was* a case or not, I suspected. An indictment would come easily. All we needed was a bare *prima facie* case. Certainly Rat had built that. Perhaps he was still building it.

I glanced up at Elena Quintero. She was speaking quietly with her minutes clerk, leaning forward over the bench. She looked very tired, almost haggard. It appeared she had simply thrown her makeup on that morning, pulled back her long dark hair and secured it with a comb. As she reached out to take a sheaf of papers from the clerk, I could see that her hand was trembling. She was carrying not just the burden of her husband dying inch by inch, but the constant and unrelenting demands of her judicial duties as well. I didn't envy her. I wondered if I could do as well if I were in her position. Then the clerk resumed his seat, and Judge Quintero gaveled the courtroom into silence.

—This court will conduct the present bail hearing in the case of *State* v. *St. Juste,* she said slowly, the depth and sharpness of her fatigue making her voice harsh and edgy. —But since the court has known the defendant socially for a number of years, trial on the case-in-chief, if there should be one, will be allotted to another division, another judge. Mr. Maitland, is the State ready?

—If it please the court, the State is ready, Maitland said, looking a little puzzled.

I heard a scuttling sound behind me and turned my head just enough to see Wes rising from his seat beyond the bar, headed for the door. I wondered why he wasn't staying for the hearing. Then, as I watched the door close behind Wes, I saw Henry Holman sitting at the end of one of the spectator's benches, a fawn-colored Stetson on his lap, his hair uncombed, what looked like a three-days' growth of beard on his pink face. His eyes were riveted on René's back as if he were powerless to look away.

By then Maitland had made his formal plea for holding René without bail, or, in the alternative, setting the bail very high. He had little hope of the first. Whatever evidence there might be against René, there was none at all to suggest that he might be a danger to himself or to others, and, beyond the gravity of the charge against him, none that he might flee to avoid prosecution.

Jock Marvell made those points quickly, concisely, in low measured tones. He asked the court to release René on his own recognizance. After all, he was a respected member of the community. Almost all of his assets were tied up in real property or business dealings of one kind or another. He had spent most of his adult life in New Orleans. There was no reason to suppose he had in mind anything other than meeting and refuting the awful charge laid against him.

Judge Quintero hardly seemed to listen. Outside an occasional nod or the jotting of a note on the papers before her, she kept her gaze focused down on the bench. It was as if her mind were elsewhere, thinking of something other than the business before the court. When Marvell was done, she was silent for what seemed a long time. Then she turned to the prosecutor's table.

—Well, Mr. Maitland? Any rebuttal?

John tried. He repeated in other language more or less what he'd said before. Finally he sat down and Elena Quintero studied her desktop once more.

—I'm going to grant bail to Mr. St. Juste, she said slowly. —The State's case to this point is essentially circumstantial. I believe fifty thousand dollars is sufficient to assure the court of his appearance. The judge to whom the case-in-chief is allotted may wish to set a hearing to change this arrangement. That will be up to him. The District Attorney may wish to submit additional evidence relating to bail later. Court is recessed for half an hour.

We stood up as she did, and I watched her leave the bench looking as if she barely had strength enough to walk the few yards back to her chambers. I supposed the pressure of her husband's final sickness was weighing heavily on her.

Maitland glanced over at René and Jock Marvell. They were shaking hands. It had been a small triumph, but in this sort of situation, every victory counts. René on bail was a man perhaps facing indictment and trial. René in jail would have been a criminal awaiting disposition.

Maitland looked drained and defeated. There was every chance that he could present the circumstances of Madeline's death to the grand jury so as to get an indictment. But meanwhile Marvell had managed it one more time. Maitland rose from the table and started out

of the courtroom without saying anything to me. I closed my briefcase and went after him.

We had almost reached the door when Henry Holman surged up out of his seat and grabbed Maitland's arm. As I drew close, I was shocked at Henry's appearance. His eyes were wide, bloodshot, and his lips were pulled back against his teeth as if he had just taken hold of his deadliest enemy.

—You let him go. You let that murdering bastard walk right out . . .

He wasn't shouting, but he wasn't quiet, either. I pushed between Maitland and Henry and took his hands in mine, trying to soothe him.

—Uncle Henry, we don't set bail. We . . .

—Is that woman on the bench bought? How about the grand jury? Somebody already paid 'em off? I want to know. I'll give 'em more . . .

—For God's sake, Mr. Holman, get yourself under control, Maitland hissed, looking to see how much notice we were getting from the courtroom crowd.

Maitland walked out of the courtroom, but I was stopped by a hand on my shoulder. It was Jock Marvell. He nodded at Henry, and then began speaking to me in a low voice.

—Since this matter is finished for now, perhaps we can reach some agreement on Santorini Malaporte's case, Denise.

They were the wrong words at the wrong moment.
—How in God's name can you defend that animal? I asked. Louder than I had intended to.

Jock Marvell didn't smile. I saw in his eyes the slightest trace of surprise. I wondered if it was possible that no one had ever asked him that question before about the bacteria and plague germs and beasts he managed to set free on the streets again. But then his expression changed. It was an attitude I'd seen often before. A woman had asked him that question. The question had arisen from her unbridled emotion. It wasn't a question, really. It required no answer. He answered anyhow. In a way.

—Have you asked Mr. Holman why he's publishing Santo's recollections in his newspaper? Don't bother. Mr. Holman is in the newspaper business. I'm in the legal defense business. I don't make the rules. I just play by them.

Henry stared at him for a moment, then nodded. He still looked distracted, but he had his voice back under control.

—That's fine, Mr. Marvell. That's a fine way of putting it. Let's do us a deal. How much is my . . . is St. Juste paying you to defend? I'll double it if you dump him.

Marvell wasn't at all surprised by that. I suspected he'd had the same offer made before.

—We haven't talked fee just yet, he told Henry.

—But it wouldn't matter. What you're asking is unethical.

Henry looked from one of us to the other, his eyes bright with anger—as if he couldn't decide which of us he found more disgusting. Then he slammed the light tan Stetson down on his head and stalked out of the courtroom.

—Let's go by Maylie's and talk over lunch, Jock was saying. —Fine martinis, a very tasty boiled beef brisket.

As lunches go, I've had worse. Maylie's has been around for much longer than I've lived, and as with so many New Orleans restaurants they'd found out what they do best and stayed with it, only refining it now and then, making wonderful a little better.

But Marvell was something else. He reminded me in his usual polite persuasive tones that if we didn't give him transactional immunity for Malaporte, Lazy Louie Donovan was going to have nothing more to worry about than a divorce action and a permanent bad name with the Orleans Parish sheriff's office. I told Marvell I'd get back to him after checking with Maitland and headed for the office. It occurred to me that I might be able to pry Maitland away from his determination to see Lazy Louie in the slam by reminding him that Marvell represented Malaporte. And this one we could win. If we allowed Donovan to turn over, his testimony would put Santo away for a long time—especially since he'd fall under the career criminals provision of the code. But I also knew that John Maitland rarely changes his mind—such as it is. Perhaps going down in flames holding one's unyielding banner aloft is a mark of aristocracy. Or is it just an indication of profound deviant stupidity?

Maitland was out. But he wanted to see me as soon as he returned to go over the St. Juste file. To decide if we really wanted to take it before the grand jury in its present state. Oh God, I thought, now he's wondering how many people he'll anger versus how many he'll please if he indicts René. Maybe he's out taking a poll this afternoon. From a table at the 4141 Club where that slender little waiter with the penciled eyebrows hovers over him.

I sat at my desk and wondered what I was doing there. I didn't have to do it, God knows. The money meant nothing. If I never worked again, I'd still be able to do anything I wanted to do, and not necessarily within reason, either. My grandfather had seen to that. He'd known what it meant to work oneself back up from near poverty to affluence. He'd learned how to make money in New Orleans, and how to hold on to it. As the last Lemoyne, all of it was mine. The good life as New Orleans understood it was mine for as long as I lived. If that was what I wanted. If that was what my life meant to me. It was my choice. I could go on carrying the family name into a third generation of lawyering: my grandfather had been a lawyer, and my father had been a district attorney. Or I could walk away from it. It was up to me.

But was it? Suppose I wanted to turn away from this wretched job, from the law, from New Orleans? What would I do? Where would I go? What about Wes and me?

Thinking about it got me nowhere. I reached for the phone and dialed Wes. I wondered if we could talk about it, if his inveterate loathing of New Orleans would allow him to see how hard it was for me to imagine stepping outside the world I'd grown up in— despite its pretensions, its flaws, its hardened arteries.

—Colvin, he said in that clipped accent that was Southern and something else at the same time. What was the clever nickname someone had come up with for his hometown? Oh yes, Shreveport, Texas. Only thirteen miles inside the Louisiana border, and straining to go west.

I could tell he was at his terminal working or had something on paper in his hands. He always sounded that way when his mind was elsewhere and he really didn't want to be disturbed.

—I'm buying tonight, I told him. —Where and when?

—Dennie, he answered, his voice softer, lower pitched. —I hear they've sprung your Cajun Casanova.

—Not mine. I have a down-home Don Juan of my own.

—Yeah, well . . .

—Do you want to feed with me or not?

—Baby, I'm tied up. There's this kind of weird thing I have to follow up on.

—You're with that scumbag Malaporte again, cackling over the time he pushed an ice pick into someone's ear.

—No, really. Malaporte's history. I finished with him a couple of days ago.

It was his lying voice. Somehow, when a man from north Louisiana is lying, his voice takes on the character of a radio revival preacher—the very symbol of honesty and rectitude among them, I suppose. Wes was with Malaporte and didn't want to get into it with me.

—Right, I said shortly. —See you around.

He was saying something else, but I dropped the receiver back on the telephone cradle. Calling him had been a bad idea, a weak idea. If I needed to think about what to do with my life—with myself—Wes Colvin might be the very last person I should talk to. For his sake as well as mine.

Maitland hadn't returned by the time I left the office. Apparently he hadn't completed his poll, or matters of more importance had detained him. It was just as well. I was in no hurry to put together the case against René. Even if he were guilty, it would still seem as if I were turning against a friend. Madeline was gone, and now René. As if there'd been an awful car accident, a plane crash. As if they'd died together.

I drove past State Street, down to Carrollton, then back into the Riverbend area where some of the most interesting shops in New Orleans are located. Ever since I'd discovered Madeline's body, I'd wanted to see Yvonne Lafleur.

Her boutique was still open, and I strolled through the interconnecting room toward the back, nodding to the salesgirls, glancing at old laces from Ireland and the new silks Yvonne had started bringing in from China. All the clothing was elegant and very feminine, as was Yvonne.

—Tea, Denise?

—I'd love some, I told Yvonne. —Somehow it seems colder this fall.

—It's wonderful for business. The cold drives people in off the street.

I laughed. If Yvonne could get them into the shop, she'd certainly sell them—anything from silk lingerie to go under the dress to the finishing touch of a hat custom-designed to complement it.

Yvonne sat down across from me and poured two cups of jasmine tea. She was dressed in a black velvet suit accented by an antique lace collar. A matching piece of lace covered the crown of her wide-brimmed hat. Her dark eyes, her smile, made me feel warmer. I'd never really thought of her boutique as a clothing store. It was a pleasant place to come and browse and keep up with what went on in those social circles my work had ruled me out of.

—It was awful about Madeline St. Juste, Yvonne said, passing a cup and saucer to me with a wedge of lemon on the side. —The two of you were close, weren't you?

—Very. She was my godmother.

—I don't believe it about René, Yvonne said matter-of-factly, her expression ever so slightly defensive. As if she expected me to take the opposite view.

—That's odd, I answered. —Neither do I.

Yvonne looked a little surprised, then nodded and dropped her voice to an even more confidential tone.

—I knew them both very well. Madeline used to come in at least once a week. In fact, the very day she . . .

Yvonne's voice faded, but I could complete the thought.

—She came here? You saw her?

—Yes. I remember, because it had been a while since I'd seen her. And because I had a customer, and she waited for me.

—How did she seem?

—Nothing out of the ordinary. Of course she looked as if she'd just thrown her clothes and makeup on, but it was mid-afternoon and I supposed . . .

—Did she buy anything?

Yvonne hesitated as if she didn't want to tell me. I tasted my tea and waited.

—She shopped for a very long time. She must have seen every nightgown and robe set in the shop. Then . . . she picked the gown . . . she died in.

—I was sure it was from here as soon as I saw it. But how do you know what she wore?

—There was some sort of description in the paper. I could tell. And I didn't know just what to feel.

—Did Madeline say anything? Anything about why she wanted such an expensive silk gown and robe?

—I think I joked with her about it. Because it wasn't really the sort of thing Madeline bought. She tended to be . . . conservative, practical. The gown was a little on the frothy side. Usually brides-to-be buy them.

—Did she say anything that might make you think

she was trying to win René back, that he was having an affair?

Yvonne's eyes widened. —No, nothing like that. But then Madeline never would have . . .

Yvonne was frowning, trying to recall. —She did say something, though. Something about . . . she wanted the gown for a play. That's it. She had a role in a play, and she'd be wearing it.

Yvonne stopped talking and put down her teacup.

—A play? I repeated. —I never knew Madeline was interested in dramatics.

—Oh, she was active in all sorts of literary affairs, Yvonne said. —She was president of the Friends of the Library for a while, then there was something with the English-Speaking Union.

—But why do you suppose she was wearing it that night?

Yvonne smiled a knowing smile. —I think your job with the district attorney's office is muddling your head, Denise. Does a woman need a reason to wear a lovely new gown?

Yvonne was probably right. There was no more to it than that. On the other hand, René never spent Friday nights at home. Then it suddenly occurred to me. Madeline might have put on her gown because she wanted to be seen in it that last night of her life.

But if that was so, by whom?

CHAPTER

11

After I left Yvonne's, I dropped by Casamento's on Magazine Street and gorged on an oyster po-boy sandwich with fries and a draft beer. The homemade bread and fresh fried oysters cheered me up. Don't ask why. I suppose it's because our spirits and bodies are tied closely together and the easing of one affects the other.

As I left, I realized that I hadn't even thought of Malaporte or René or Madeline as I ate. For the first time in a long time, I'd eaten alone and been alone. With myself. I was feeling better when I turned the Mercedes around and started back to State Street.

The era of good feeling didn't last long. When I pulled into the drive, a car was there ahead of me. In the dark, I didn't recognize it. Just some long anonymous sedan that looked deserted. Then the driver's door opened, and René St. Juste was standing in my headlights. Smiling.

—René, I said, as I fumbled for my keys, —what are

you thinking? You shouldn't be here without counsel. In fact, you shouldn't be here at all.

René smiled, took my key, and opened the door. Then he stood there silently.

—All right, I said, unable to send him away and close the door. —One quick drink.

We went into the library, and René walked to the bar. He knew the house as well as I did. He and my grandfather had enjoyed one another's company. Years ago, they had gone duck hunting together in the marshes near Delacroix Island every winter. Now he was mixing old-fashioneds in his own special way. I tossed some logs on the muted fire and turned up the lamp on the library table.

As he handed me a drink, he looked at me in silence for a moment. —You don't believe any of this, do you? I mean . . .

—I . . . have no opinion yet. I'm waiting.

—Someone planted that earring, Dennie, he said. —I didn't take Madeline's jewelry.

—You need money, don't you? A lot of money.

He started to answer, then stopped, shrugged. I knew he had decided that a lie would be useless.

—You could say that. Most of my money is in mineral options. With oil and gas on the rise, they'd be worth millions.

—But oil and gas aren't rising. They're giving leases away.

—Yes, and if I can't hold on to the options . . .

—You'll lose it all.

—At the end of it? I'll be . . . a little better off than that boy who came in from the parish, out of the swamps.

—And you can't bear the thought of that?

His face grew dark, his eyes uncertain, confused.

—I don't know what I can bear, Dennie. I thought

what I've accomplished, the position I've built here in
New Orleans, meant the world to me. But everything's
falling down. Friends are turning against me. . . . Earlier
tonight I called Al and Mignon Darcy, some of our old-
est and best friends. I thought drinks, dinner. I'm still
on the streets, not behind bars. A very small celebration for that at least. They said . . . they were tied up. I
asked about tomorrow night. Finally Mignon told me
they thought it best if we didn't get together until all
this . . . beastliness is over.

His shoulders slumped, and he put his head in his
hands. I thought I understood. René had always been a
physical man, a man who made his way by force of
body and personality, through his energy, his drive. He
had made friends—and enemies—pushing and surg-
ing ahead. People had always been taken with those
qualities in him. Now even those who should know
him best wondered if perhaps he'd turned that force
loose on Madeline. Now he was involved in things that
had nothing to do with personality, energy, laughter,
and good fellowship. The oil and gas market on which
his living depended had fallen apart because of the stupidity and venality of men five thousand miles away.
The courts, much closer, had begun the slow deliberate
process of trying him, testing him, to discover whether
he had killed. And he could touch, charm, disarm none
of what stood against him. René lifted his eyes to mine
and began to speak in a soft strengthless voice.

—In the old days in France, when you were convicted of a capital crime but somehow managed to
dodge the snap of Madame Guillotine, before you were
transported in chains, shipped like dead meat to Devil's
Island or the Guyanas, there was a ceremony. They
told you you were dead. Your property was passed on
to your heirs, your name was removed from state

records. In all legal matters thereafter, you became one of . . . *les mortes.* They called it "civil death." I know what it must have felt like. . . .

—Perhaps your lady friend . . . I said cruelly, wishing before the words were out that I had said nothing.

René looked up quickly, without accusation. —No. I can't see her now. I won't. The damned police are hoping for that. They think she's . . . some kind of motive. She's not. She's . . . bearing her own anguish.

He reached across the table and took my hand. I didn't pull it away. My last thoughtless remark had disarmed me somehow.

—Dennie, I need someone to believe in me. I don't need your help. Marvell's a clever lawyer. I need . . .

René looked away, a half-smile on his lips.

—On the way over here, I was remembering your first dance. Do you?

For just a moment, I couldn't call to mind what he meant. Then it came back with a rush.

It had been some absurd dinner dance given by aspiring society mothers for girls who in those days were still called "subdebs." Madeline was there, trying to do the right thing for me, and I was dying. We were, most of us, thirteen and fourteen, and even those who would in a matter of months begin to become attractive women were still gawky and homely with hair that wouldn't be managed, braces that couldn't come off yet, flat breasts, and straight legs. Still, we had all bought new long dresses and spent a sleepless night in excited fantasies involving tall strangers who swept us away to the accompaniment of violins.

But the boys who were invited were only too well known and had hardly grown past the toad-and-snake-bearing age. They ignored the girls and ran around the tiny ballroom hooting and laughing, fighting, rolling on the floor until Dudley Keagan, a fat ugly boy whom everyone despised, got knocked into the punch bowl and screamed out against his tormenters one word at the top of his lungs:

MOTHERFUCKERS!

The whole place fell silent. Then René, who had just come in to help with the chaperoning, walked over and whispered something to Dudley, and something to the other boys. The boys nodded and became quiet. Then René came over and took my hand. I knew I was dying for certain.

—I . . . can't dance, I said.

—You've had all manner of lessons, Madeline told me sharply. —Of course you can dance.

—No I can't, I said. —If you make me go out there, I'm going to throw up. I mean it.

—No you're not, René said. —Come on.

He dragged me across the floor with everyone watching and said something to the orchestra leader, a faded little man with thin colorless hair in a tuxedo that was worn as smooth and bright as if it were lacquer instead of cloth. The man smiled and nodded, and the orchestra began to play. It was a waltz, I remembered. Not Strauss or Lanner. Something more recent, something romantic and lovely, with violins, called "Tenderly."

Then René lifted me from the floor. He whirled me around as if I were made of meringue or cotton candy. Forgetting that the whole room was watching us, I found myself dancing, following him, moving on my own as if I had been born in the midst of a waltz.

In a few moments, I realized that the others had begun coming out on the floor, too. That those nasty stupid little boys were asking other girls to dance, and that the disastrous party, if not a triumph, was at least saved.

And I had realized something else. Something that I must have repressed almost as soon as it had risen from the well of mere feeling to the level of consciousness.

I had realized that René was the most attractive man I had ever known, and that being in his arms was something other than a moment's diversion. I wanted to be in his arms. I wanted to stay there, to grow there, warm and protected and . . . something else. *Oh God*, I thought later that night in the dark as I lay in bed playing the evening over and over in my mind, *Oh God, what would it be like to . . . sleep with René?*

—You were lovely, René said softly. —You didn't know you were. You weren't going to know it for another year or so. But you already were.

—When the boys were fighting . . . you made them stop. They behaved the rest of the evening. What did you say to them?

René sipped his drink. —They were smart boys, he said. —They're doctors and lawyers and bankers now. That pitiful fat lump who fell against the punch bowl is a psychiatric resident. Imagine that.

—But . . .

—I told them what all bad little boys want to hear, that I'd kick their fucking heads in if they didn't behave, and treat the young ladies nicely.

—That's all?

—It was the truth. They knew it was. They just needed someone to calm them down, to remind them of their duty to the girls.

I studied René for a long moment. His smile had faded. I wondered if he was still remembering that night when we had danced.

—You really love women, don't you?

He looked up from his drink. This time the smile was

ironic. —I suppose I do, he said. —Despite . . . this, despite everything.

He rose then, found his coat and started out of the library. —I'll be going now, he said softly. —I just needed to be with someone who . . . believes in me.

I followed him into the foyer. The light there was brighter, and René's face looked thinner, gray under his tan.

—You're going to find out I had nothing to do with Madeline's death, he said slowly.

—I hope so, I told him quietly. And I meant it.

—You will. Maybe not right away, but you will. Because a lie like that can't stand forever.

—René . . .

—You'll see, he said. Then he took me in his arms and kissed me.

I think I must have wanted him to for a long time. Despite the situation, it felt right. Then he opened the door and was gone.

I drew a deep breath and snapped off the downstairs lights. Then for a moment I stood looking out the glass panes of my front door into the yard bathed in cold blue light from the street lamp beyond. I had always been a little in love with René, more attracted to him than I wanted to acknowledge. I wondered if it were nothing more than that buried feeling that forced me to believe he hadn't killed Madeline. Then outside it began to sleet, and I turned and walked upstairs.

The next morning was overcast and grim once more. As I looked out my bedroom window, I saw a patina of frost on the tile roof just below. I shivered and pulled on brown tights instead of stockings and added a soft tan cashmere sweater vest under my suit coat for warmth.

Downstairs Carole had set a light breakfast on the glass table in the solarium, and I was studying my glass of orange juice and thinking of the beaches in Bermuda when the front door chimes sounded. In a moment, Wes came in, kissed my cheek, and sat down across from me. He looked very tired, and his hair was damp from the freezing rain that still fell outside. For a moment he said nothing as Carole brought him coffee.

—English muffin, Mr. Colvin?

—No thanks, Carole, he said. —But maybe you could bring the coffeepot.

—Sorry. Every two cups is brewed fresh.

—Ah...

—Did you and Santorini have a pleasant evening? I asked him, trying to keep the acid in my voice under control.

He shook his head as if he was weary of having to tell me the same thing over and over. I wondered if I was beginning to sound like a suspicious wife.

—I had something else on yesterday.

—Did you really?

Then his smile broke through and I realized that he'd been working to keep it in ever since he walked into the room.

—You want to know where I was, what I was up to?

He pulled a newspaper out of the side pocket of his raincoat and spread it on the table. The second headline jumped out at me:

JUDGE IN ST. JUSTE CASE MET
DEFENDANT IN QUARTER APARTMENT

At first it made no sense. I understood the words, but they seemed no more than a grammatical fit.

—What in God's name...? I began.

—Read it, babe... and look at the picture.

My eyes moved from the headline to a sharp photo of Elena Quintero standing in front of René's St. Ann Street apartment, key in hand, opening the door. My eyes must have been the size of saucers as I stared over at Wes.

—Gotcha, he said grinning. —When Trapp sees this, he's gonna go down for the third time.

—I don't believe it. It's just . . . not possible.

—See? That's why you should give up this prosecutor's work. You're not cynical. You don't believe anything's possible if it's not right. But it *is* possible. She's a woman, he's a man—in New Orleans, even that wouldn't matter. They've been shacking up for months.

Wes rubbed his hands and drank his coffee. —I can't wait to see Rat. He's gonna piss and moan and ask why I didn't bring it to him.

I was reading the article then, and it seemed solid. Wes had spoken to others who lived in the building, had shown them pictures of Elena Quintero. Yes, she was seen frequently there. On Fridays, weekends. A very lovely, quiet lady. The other tenants thought she was foreign, that the apartment belonged to her and her Latin husband. They had no idea who she was, no idea at all of a connection between the attractive couple who seemed to spend very little time in their French Quarter apartment and a murder in Uptown New Orleans.

When I was done, I shook my head. It wasn't a connection I'd have ever made. Perhaps Wes was right. Perhaps whatever this job called for, I didn't have.

—How did you . . . ?

Wes was on his second cup of coffee. Carole stood behind him, looking over at the paper I'd dropped on the table.

—At his bail hearing, the judge said she knew St. Juste.

—Half the people in New Orleans know him.

Wes laughed. —You mean half the people who live Uptown between Jackson and Carrollton, Tchoupitoulas and Claiborne, and even then . . .

—All right, I said shortly. —You've made your point.

—I just connected a missing love interest and a lady who looked troubled when she had to preside over that hearing.

—Her husband's dying, I told him.

—Ain't we all? Never mind. Maybe all my thinking was wrong, but I got where I was going. When she said she was going to recuse herself . . .

—You didn't go down to the Quarter and stand in front of that apartment building?

—Nope. It happens that Judge Quintero's secretary owed me a favor.

—What? Why?

—Well, Counselor, it goes back a ways. Priss Wyman, she's the secretary, has a son. The son used to do dope. The cops had him made for some two-bit retailing . . .

—And you sat on the story till it died?

—I do that sometimes. She raised the kid alone. She's always done the best she could. He knows better now. Rat and I got into it and shook it around a year or so ago.

—So it was pay-up time.

Wes raised his hands and tried to look innocent.

—All I wanted to know was how well our lady judge knew René St. Juste. What the hell, there's Gonzo reporting, too. Priss told me he never came by the courthouse, but he usually called during Quintero's lunch break on Fridays. She knew, because sometimes the judge was stuck in court and she'd take the call.

Wes sat back as Carole poured him fresh coffee. —I knew then I was home. I could have carried it myself after that, but . . .

—You had a little more interest to collect.

—She told me the messages were always peculiar, cryptic. Like, Tell the judge Mr. St. Juste said the settlement was acceptable, or no, he couldn't accept the terms. But Priss knew the bastard didn't have any business before the court. Shit, I could do better than that dead drunk. Anyhow, I asked the secretary to pass on one more message, the positive one.

—Oh, God, you left word René wanted to see her. . . . You set her up.

—She set herself up, Dennie. And I was there with a hot camera and fast film. I've got everything but a motion picture of her going in and coming out of the St. Ann Street apartment.

—She must have been horrified when she realized . . .

—Play bad, you gotta lose. Now the whole damned case is gonna open up. Maybe she'll be taking a trip upriver with old Renny-baby.

—She's already recused herself from the case, Wes.

He looked at me in astonishment. —Recused . . . ? Goddamnit, she ought to have been standing beside him being arraigned. How do you know who pulled the trigger on Madeline St. Juste?

—I don't, and neither do you.

—We're getting a bigger slate of candidates. Maybe René *didn't* do it. Maybe he was covering for his judicial squeeze. Maybe . . .

I felt my face burning. All I could think of was the

waste, the pain. Now Elena Quintero was drawn into it along with René and Henry Holman and the rest of us.

—You seem to have a scorched-earth policy, I told Wes.

—What the hell is that supposed to mean?

—Anything goes. Now Elena Quintero's career is wrecked. For what? Because she and René . . .

Wes's eyes narrowed. I knew that look. Redneck Moralist. He and Rat could have done some simply wonderful piecework for Savonarola, or Cromwell, or Cotton Mather.

I didn't know what had passed between Elena Quintero and René St. Juste, but nothing short of conclusive evidence was going to make me believe that either of them had murdered Madeline in cold blood, or any other temperature of blood, for that matter. There was something else. Something touching those last pieces of clothing Madeline had bought at Yvonne Lafleur's.

Was it just possible that there was more to this case than we'd even considered yet? Someone nameless and faceless who had come to the St. Juste house that night? Someone Madeline had expected?

—You were saying something, Wes said, breaking into my thoughts.

—What?

—I think you were gonna tell me what a sonofabitch I am for blowing the whistle on René's chippy.

I think I must have stared at him as if we'd never met.

—Elena Quintero is no . . . chippy.

Wes shrugged. There were good women and bad women. Bad women slept around, and if they were married that made them very bad indeed.

—I'm sure you and Henry had drinks over the story, I went on.

—He thought it was good reporting, Wes said flatly, his control not covering the anger in his voice. —The old man's hurting, but he's hanging in there. He wants St. Juste to burn. I don't blame him.

—I'm sure you don't. And while Henry's hanging in there, who else is going to hang? You've taken care of Elena Quintero. Who's next?

—Goddamn, Wes said, slamming his cup down into the saucer. —What the hell is it with you? You're supposed to be a prosecutor. Someone murdered the goddamned woman who raised you. You ought to be singing hallelujah over my story. Nailing Quintero blows away all St. Juste's defenses. Now you can prove he had a motive—with a name on it.

—No, you've got a bylined story. Elena Quintero has a ruined career and a husband who's going to die now with more pain than cancer gives. I don't know that it will mean anything to the case against René.

Wes's face darkened. He got up from the table and stared at me, his eyes cold, distant. Ah, I thought I could hear Madeline whispering, you've crossed him when the blood-madness is playing in his veins. He won't forgive that. None of them do. Not Henry, not René, not Rat. Not John Wesley Colvin either.

—You don't give a shit if he's guilty or not, do you?

—I believe he's innocent . . . until proven guilty.

—No use in going on with this, Wes said with suppressed anger, and started to turn away.

—I'm not sure there's any use in us going on with anything, I heard myself saying, feeling even as I spoke a terrible emptiness suddenly present in my stomach, my lungs.

—What the hell is that supposed to mean? he asked.

—I'm not sure, I told him. —When I am, you'll be the first to know.

CHAPTER
12

Marj was looking pie-eyed when I walked into the bullpen we call an office after the coldest, loneliest drive across town I'd made in a very long time.

—In the conference room . . .

I frowned and checked the date on my watch.

—There's no office meeting today. Are you trying to psyche me?

—No, I mean . . . *she's* in there. Waiting.

—Marj, who in God's name are you talking about?

—The lady judge. The one in the *Item*. The one Wes caught at it.

Elena Quintero. I'd forgotten her in the heat—or cold—of Wes's leave-taking. All the way across town I'd been investigating my feelings, my motives, my fears. I hadn't even thought about the pretext for our quarrel. I hadn't even considered what I'd tell Maitland when he came to me about the story. Now she was waiting a few steps away, and it appeared she hadn't asked to see Maitland. I could understand that. My court appearance at the arraignment made me a legitimate contact in the D.A.'s office. Perhaps she thought she'd receive an easier hearing from me. I hoped she was right—and it occurred to me that I hoped she didn't know that Wes and I were engaged. It wasn't something I felt proud of just then.

—Hold calls, I told Marj, —and keep people out of that room. I mean *everyone.*

—I can't tell Good Hood...

—You tell him I'd appreciate his discretion. I'll check in with him when I'm through.

—Okay, but...

—And no one finds out who I'm with. I mean it, Marj. That goes for Theresa in Screening and Rita in Pre-Sentence... no one.

Marj nodded, her eyes still the size of cupcakes, and I drew a deep breath and walked into the conference room.

Elena Quintero looked beautiful, almost regal. She was seated at the long conference table, her hands folded before her, the flowing lines of her deep burgundy dress and matching coat obscuring her femininity much as her judicial robes did when she presided in court. But her face was drawn and pale under the deep warm tan complexion that didn't require weeks in Florida to keep up, and she rose nervously to her feet when I came in and closed the door behind me.

—Miss Lemoyne...

—Your Honor...

—You'll have seen the *Item* this morning?

—Yes.

—Let me start by saying I've taken a leave of absence from the bench until this matter is resolved. Then I

172 A CIVIL DEATH

should say how sorry, how very sorry I am that I didn't come forward at the start. It might have made everything . . . simpler.

—I think so.

—And finally, I'm prepared to answer any questions you or the police may have for me.

I nodded and studied her, wondering if I could possibly be as self-contained in her situation. Looking at Elena Quintero just then, I realized what breeding meant—however or wherever she had come by it.

—I'm sorry things have come to this, I told her. —I've always admired you, your work.

Her smile was short, perfunctory. —It was a long hard road coming up, she said softly. —I suspect the way down may be much shorter.

—I'll need to speak to Captain Trapp before . . . You understand?

—Of course. Shall I wait here?

—For a few minutes. I'll ask him to come over.

Elena Quintero's brow wrinkled. —I'm not asking for special treatment, she said. —If we should go to Central Lockup . . .

—You're not a suspect, I told her. —You've volunteered as a witness. I won't be long.

At least I hoped I wouldn't be as I stepped out of the conference room and headed for my desk. Marj was watching me as if she thought I might be about to tell all. I ignored her and dialed Rat's private line. It would catch him in the office, in his car, or at his apartment. It rang several times. Then he answered, and I breathed a short sigh of relief. I hoped getting hold of him wouldn't turn out to be the easiest part.

—Trapp here.

—Why haven't you been calling me? I asked.

—Ah, my Uptown dumpling. Why, honey, I called all night, every fifteen minutes, but see . . .

—You haven't seen the morning paper.

—What are you saying, woman? I read it through at the Pontchartrain Coffee Shop. After my customary morning run.

—Then why didn't you . . . ?

—Priorities, Counselor. We had this guy with a sawed-off shotgun try to make an unscheduled withdrawal from the First National Bank about an hour ago. Dusted some folks, made off with a bundle . . . all manner of shit.

—Was anyone . . . ?

—Killed? No, dearest. Nobody that counts. The bad man holed up inside a little frame house over on Frenchman Street. Told the family in there they was all gonna go out together. Some cop caught him plumb in the face with a .357 AP. Right through the wall of the house, if you believe it.

—Oh, God, I believe it. Anyone I know?

—The bad man? I don't reckon. I believe you and he moved in different circles.

—I mean the shooter.

—Ah, well, as to that . . .

—I thought so. Are you still on the scene?

—I just got back to the office, finished my report, cleaned and reloaded old Roger, and I'm ready for action. Would you like to ease on by criminal court with me?

—No need. She's over here, Rat.

—Ah . . .

—It's terrible, and she's very brave.

—Ummm. So was the Blitz and so was the Luftwaffe,

Counselor. Why don't you back off that till we can stoke a fire under the lady and boil out the truth?

—There's no call for that. She says she'll answer anything we ask.

—That's mighty white of her, Dennie. But don't let it fuck up your head. Remember Lazy Louie?

—What has that creep to do with...?

—Your lady judge might have planned this whole business with St. Juste. Things happen like that.

—Oh, hell. That's what Wes said this morning.

—You seen my man? I'm gonna pull off his head and spit down his neck when I catch up to him, you know. That jive-ass bastard could have *shared*...

—Rat, do me a favor. I ran Wes off this morning. I don't know if we'll ever be on again. I don't want to argue with you, too.

—Last thing on my mind, sweetness. But you got to realize that your judge over there is in the soup. And it ain't Campbell's. She brewed her own. Hell, maybe it wasn't any kind of plot at all. Maybe she went over there to have it out with Madeline St. Juste, got upset, and jerked her string. Maybe that fool St. Juste is covering for *her*. I've heard that happens, too.

—This is a replay. Do you and Wes have a group mind you share?

—We been to Hollywood, we been to Redwood. Both still looking for a heart of gold. Maybe Madeline told Quintero that the whistle was fixing to blow on her with all the Uptown folks. Reckon that could be why Madeline St. Juste was all dolled up that night?

—No, I don't, I said firmly. —No woman would receive her husband's mistress in her own bedroom. Ugh.

There was silence on the other end. Then I heard Rat sigh. —Now you see? You are a pure education to me.

What you say sounds right, but I'd have never figured it on my own. Keep the judge company, sugar. I'm on my way.

Rat was on his best behavior. He wore a charcoal suit, a white shirt with a scarlet, black, and white regimental tie, and spoke very softly. It was hard to believe that a little while ago he had killed a man.

Yes, Elena acknowledged, she'd been with René the evening of Madeline's death. They'd met at the apartment as usual. René had been upset because there'd been a fearful argument that morning. Madeline had known he was having an affair. She'd known it was Elena and was outraged. How could René? Of all the women he had to choose from, why her?

—What exactly did St. Juste tell you about the quarrel with his wife? Rat asked.

—René told Madeline he wanted a divorce. She said she'd see him in hell before she turned him loose for a . . .

Elena stopped and lowered her head, her eyes on the conference table as she remembered.

—Sounds like Mrs. St. Juste had it in special for you, Rat said. —Like . . . anybody but you. Is that so?

Elena raised her eyes and nodded. —In 1965, my family came here from Cuba. I was sixteen. We'd always lived well in Cuba. My father was a doctor there. Here, he was nothing. In the old days, I'd have gone abroad to a university. But . . . as it was, I took a job as a maid to help out.

—You worked for . . . Madeline?

Elena smiled at me. —I was Maria Elena Sanchez then.

I stared, trying to see in her the trim friendly Latin maid who'd worked briefly for Madeline long ago.

—I remember you as a small girl, Denise. You were very lonely, weren't you? Madeline St. Juste helped. She was a selfish woman, but she cared for you.

—How long did you work for the St. Justes? Rat said.

—Only a little while. René was kind to me. He made me feel that I wasn't simply another . . . appliance in the house.

—Ah, Rat breathed. —But it didn't work so well with Mrs. St. Juste?

Elena's jaw tightened. —Madeline St. Juste was a consummate bitch to me. She couldn't believe that René's kindness had any object but . . .

—Did it? I asked.

She looked at me with sudden distaste. —Yes, she said, separating each word as if she feared I might not understand. —Yes, it did. René never approached me that way. And later, after Madeline made it impossible for me to stay, René and I remained . . . friends.

Rat and I looked at one another. Was his cynicism infecting me—or did I have a plentiful supply of my own that rose at the most inopportune times? Elena saw the look as it passed between us.

—René said . . . you believed in him, she said to me almost angrily.

—I don't believe he killed Madeline, I told her coolly.

—That doesn't constitute blanket immunity. He's always liked women. Any woman who's ever met him knows that.

—You think so? Perhaps René responds in the way women want him to respond.

Very nice, I thought, and more on target than you know, considering my reminiscences of last night. But I'm not defending, Judge. You are.

—So you stayed in touch, Rat said, his eyes moving back and forth between us.

—More than that, Elena said. —Doesn't it occur to either of you to wonder how I managed to pay my way through Newcomb and Tulane Law on a maid's salary?

—Ah, Rat said again. It was occurring to him just then. —You're telling us that Mr. St. Juste helped you with tuition and ...

—He paid for my schooling, Elena said simply. —After I graduated, it took me five years to pay him back, but I did. Every cent. When we met again, nothing was owed—except gratitude and ...

—Love, I said.

—You can't owe love, Elena said, almost contemptuously.

—All right, Judge, Rat cut in sharply. —You're telling me St. Juste met you at sixteen, kept up with you after his wife let you go. Then he paid for you to go to college for seven years. And in all that time he never ... ?

—The answer is no, Captain, Elena said, her voice ragged. The strain was beginning to tell on her. Her hands, clasped together on the tabletop, gripped one another tightly.

—Pardon me, ma'am, but, see, I come up in a harder school. Is that kind of thing customary amongst ... better people?

Elena laughed as if Rat's contrivedly naïve question had broken the tension.

—I don't think so, Captain. I suppose it's happened before, but I doubt it's statistically significant.

Rat grinned at her. —That makes me feel better, Judge. For a minute, I was wondering if we lived in different worlds. Instead of just different neighborhoods.

—You broke it off with René that night? I asked.

—I told him we shouldn't see one another until the situation with Madeline was resolved.

—Ummm, Rat said, almost to himself. —Reckon that gave Mr. St. Juste some incentive to ... resolve the situation?

Elena looked at him squarely. —René didn't kill Madeline.

—Then he was with you at the St. Ann Street apartment? You didn't leave until late? I put in.

She shook her head slowly. —I wish to God that were so. I wish I could say it and mean it, but there've been enough lies, haven't there?

Rat nodded and unwrapped one of his long Marsh-Wheeling cigars. He bit off the end and stared at it.

—Yeah, he said at last. —I believe we can pass on the cooked-up stories. So what time did you leave St. Ann Street?

—Seven, seven-thirty, perhaps. After court adjourned, we met as usual. We talked, we had drinks. I left.

—You went home? I asked.

—No. I'd told Paul ... my husband, that I'd be working late. So I went back to my chambers and worked until ten or ten-thirty. No, that's not so. I don't suppose I got half an hour's work done. I sat there at my desk and tried to imagine ever being happy again. You see, that evening when I left René, I thought things were as bad as they could get.

—Anyone see you at the courthouse?

—I doubt it. I have my own keys. I use the staff elevator ...

—But your husband can testify you got home like ... eleven?

Elena didn't answer for a moment. Her hands unfolded and gripped the edge of the table. I saw tears start up in her eyes, but she forced them down again.

—No . . . because . . . because . . . late last night, he slipped into a coma. The doctors tell me he won't be awakening again.

I should have expressed my sympathy, I suppose, but I didn't. Instead Elena heard me breathe a sigh of relief. She turned and tried to smile. She knew exactly what I was thinking.

—I feel the same way, Denise. He didn't see . . . this morning's *Item*.

—That's a good thing, Rat said, his voice harsh with his own emotion. —A man ought to go quiet, with it all made up in the world, made up in himself.

She broke then, and the tears came despite her control.

—It doesn't matter to either of you, and it doesn't even matter to him now, but in the years we've been married, I never . . . not ever before . . .

—Rat, I said, —I mean, Captain Trapp, can we cut this short . . . ?

He looked over at me, and his dark eyes were clear and hard and unyielding. —Not yet, Counselor. Not just yet.

Then he turned back to Elena Quintero. —I expect you've had a nurse with him, huh? What about the nurse? She would have seen you come in.

—She'd dozed off. I saw her when I came into the room and kissed Paul good night, but he was resting well and I didn't wake her.

—Ummmm . . .

Surprise came into Elena's eyes. For the first time she realized that Rat was considering the possibility that she, not René, had shot Madeline.

—Perhaps you'd better read me my rights, Captain, she said softly.

—Oh no, Judge. That would be . . . premature. See, all I've got just now is that you can't account for your time after seven-thirty. That's not a whole lot, is it?

The cynicism of Elena's look matched Rat's.

—No, she said, —it's not a lot. But it's a beginning, isn't it?

—Yes, ma'am. It's a beginning.

—One more thing, I said quickly. —Did René ever say anything that might lead you to think he'd . . . kill Madeline?

—I think I've already answered that.

—Oh no, Rat said slyly. —You said you didn't *believe* Mr. St. Juste killed his wife. But then you couldn't know that. Unless you were with him at the time of her death. Or unless you know who did kill her.

Elena took a deep breath. —He never said anything that would bear that interpretation. Nothing. He was concerned for her.

—I'm sure he was, Rat smiled politely.

After Elena Quintero had left the conference room, I walked with Rat back to his office.

—Everybody's talking, he said. —But nobody's saying anything.

—Maybe they're both telling the truth, I answered. —Maybe we're looking in all the wrong places.

—Now what the hell is that supposed to mean?

—That new gown Madeline was wearing, the robe. I checked, and she bought them at Yvonne Lafleur's the day she died.

—Women buy stuff all the time.

—Madeline hadn't. Not in months. And she said something peculiar to Yvonne.

—All right.

—She said she was going to wear them . . . in a play.

Rat looked up. —She said what?

—She told Yvonne she . . . had a role in a play.

—Role in a play . . . Was she into that kind of thing?

—Not so far as I know.

—Maybe she meant something else. You know, all the world's a stage and . . .

I shook my head. —No, but I've been wondering if Madeline decided two could play at adultery, wondering if that was the play she had a part in.

Rat looked unimpressed as he drew on his cigar and sent a warm blue jet of smoke toward the high ceiling of the hallway.

—I think you're reaching, he said. —I mean, like the lady said a play . . . a drama . . . not a one-night stand.

—What if the lady had lost all hope as far as her marriage was concerned? I asked. —What if she'd hit a few bars in the Quarter on those long empty afternoons? The Absinthe House, the Monteleone . . .

—Found her a special friend . . . ?

—And invited him home on an evening she knew René wouldn't be there . . . because he was with *his* special friend.

—Ummm . . .

—So she bought new things and had her evening planned. But he wasn't a nice man.

Rat looked away as I talked, chewing on his cigar, squinting at the fluorescent lights above.

—You saying there might be somebody we haven't tagged 'cause we don't even know he exists?

—More or less.

—It won't slide.

—Why?

—For one thing, that piece of jewelry we found in René's little place.

Rat was right. If Madeline had somehow gotten involved with a psychopath, he might have tried to make murder look like robbery by stealing her jewelry, but he *couldn't* have planted Madeline's stolen earring in René's apartment. No one but René and Elena—and maybe Madeline—knew of its existence.

We reached his office then, and Rat settled behind his desk, chin propped on his large hands, cigar between his fingers.

—See, Rat said, —things are most nearly always about the way they seem. If the fucker waddles like a duck, quacks like a duck, and lays duck eggs . . .

—It's probably a pelican, I cut in.

Rat laughed. —How about a goddamn turkey, and René St. Juste is it. Take it like it is, honey. Don't go trying to invent yourself a whole new kind of bird.

—You're probably right, but I want a look at Madeline's diary, I told Rat.

—Ah, he said as he reached behind his desk. —So you want a look at Mrs. St. Juste's diary, huh? How much time you got?

—What?

From a large pasteboard box Rat drew out a plastic trashbag. As he set it down on his desk, he began pulling out one leather-covered volume after another.

—It starts in 1957, he said slyly, —and comes right on up to that Friday. That lady liked to communicate with herself.

—Have you read any of it?

—Just the last few entries.

—I want to read all of them, I told him.

Rat looked startled. —You mean the whole goddamned thing?

—Maybe there's something . . .

—Oh, sweet thing, they haven't taught you how to clear a caseload, have they?

—There's probably nothing . . . still . . .

Rat hefted the trashbag and passed it to me.

—Sign one of those green slips on your way out. Got to keep the chain of evidence unbroken, you know.

—Whether there is any evidence or not?

He grinned as I started out of the office.

—Yeah, he said. —You know me. By the book.

I laughed. —*Your* book.

—Well . . .

CHAPTER

13

After supper, I tried to think of things I had to do, but there was nothing. I was faced with that long rank of diaries that my godmother had left behind, never supposing that, of all people, I would be reading them.

I began at the beginning, and it was surprising to learn that Madeline Holman St. Juste had shared the same hopes and fears and feelings that I had felt twenty-five years later. There were pages on dances and parties and music and boys, on long summers across Lake Pontchartrain in the Holman place outside Mandeville.

The endless round of fetes and balls and cocktail parties and debutante events around Carnival was described in detail alongside happenings in the world that Madeline had noticed, but which had meant much less to her than her escort for the next dance, or who had cut in and asked most improperly that she abandon her date and leave the party with him.

She mentioned the launching of the first Russian satellite in the same breath with a cautionary tale of Milly Darian's drinking too many Brandy Alexanders at a Christmas party. She had played "My Prayer" by the Platters over and over again until she fell asleep and awoke late in the night to hear the needle's patterned scratching at the record's end.

Madeline had loved poetry and drama. It seemed that she had always hoped that one fine day she'd awaken to find she had the gift to transform her best and deepest feelings into verse, or to convert her imaginings into plays:

There's something very special in watching a play. I know that the life lived on the stage is only a dream no different from my own daydreams. The actors live their own lives, and yet somehow they take on other lives—lives that were never really lived—and make them true. Daddy took me to see Cyrano *at the Saenger Theatre. I suppose it was just a very ordinary road company, and yet I cried for him, and for his love, and for the foolish girl who couldn't see past the end of his nose.*

I was surprised at the breadth of Madeline's reading, and at the bits and pieces she chose to write down and remember. Much of it was ordinary, banal, the sort of thing that attracts one to the saying more than what is said—silliness like Emerson's "A foolish consistency is the hobgoblin of little minds," or Santayana's "Those who cannot remember the past are condemned to repeat it." But there were better things. When she was barely seventeen, Madeline had come across something that had affected her deeply. It was from a passage of Spinoza: "Those who love God must not expect to be loved by Him in return." Madeline had been horrified by that. How could it be that the Maker of Love did not share in it? It seemed Madeline had believed that love was a contract: I give in order that you give.

She had been one of those young women who had accepted the traditional view of things almost without question. In only one area did Madeline's attitudes seem to stray seriously from the Uptown fold: she loathed the limp-wristed boys or the sleek, muscled dolts from what she ironically referred to as "the better families." They failed to interest her.

She had always been looking for a certain kind of man, someone who could break through the encrusted conventions of New Orleans society, someone who could thrill her, make her feel alive. One day her prince would come, and the two of them would reign over Uptown, cushioned by Holman money, carried forward by their verve and energy. Within decent limits, of course.

I put down the diary and poured myself a brandy. The house was silent. All I could hear was the faint fall of rain against the library window. As I sipped my drink, I tried to imagine Madeline as she must have been at my age.

Had she been bright, happy, living carefree in the fortress of Henry's money and the good opinion of her friends? Surely she had been, with nothing to break the rhythm but that romantic whisper of a love that would one day come along in the ripeness of time. Till then there were horses and yachts on the lake, summer dances and winter balls. There was no end of things to keep a young woman enthralled by her singular good fortune, the luck to be a pretty Uptown New Orleans girl of a good and well-to-do family in the late 1950s and early 1960s.

By then I'd reached the fifth volume. There was an awful disorienting feeling when I reached the entry for

November 22, 1963. She had graduated from Newcomb the year before and was working as a reporter for the *Item*—something I had never known about. The assignments editor had sent her to do a piece on the Louisiana seafood industry, and she'd equipped herself as if she were going on safari: jodhpurs, a hat with mosquito-netting, a silk blouse with long sleeves that was customed-tailored to her figure.

Then she had driven down to Delacroix Island in St. Bernard Parish to meet a pair of old men at the Gulf Outlet who had been shrimping in the waters of Bastian Bay and Oak River and Lake Borgne for decades. They would show her old Louisiana, the primordial ground of fishing, hunting, and trapping that had been opened over two centuries before by political exiles from Canadian Acadia, who had come over the generations to be called Cajuns.

It had been a bright cold day on the open waters of the bays and inlets. She had talked to the old men and learned their ways, the awful labor that is required to fill the hold of a shrimp boat and the small profit they gained from it even in a good year. Madeline had thrown off her hat and pitched in to help draw the nets aboard, to throw back trash fish, to separate out crabs and trout and redfish that could be sold at the dockside market along with the shrimp.

Then, in the evening, as the temperature dropped sharply and her thin khaki jacket had to be supplemented by a blanket one of the old men gave her, they moved slowly, silently, through the shadows back toward their home port where clusters of other aging boats put up until the early hours of the next morning when they would go out again.

There on the Delacroix docks as the sun faded out of sight, she met him. René Michel St. Juste, tall and smiling, himself moments past a long day on an oyster boat, come to help the old men unload, one of them his uncle, his mother's brother. He had lifted huge metal baskets of shrimp and fish from the boat, had hosed it down as the old men broke out a bottle of red wine and began the evening's drinking. Then he had smiled at Madeline, his white teeth bright in the twilight, the muscles in his arms rippling as he finished his work. Would she eat with him, have a drink before she drove back to New Orleans? There was a small place nearby where the fried trout and shrimp and oysters were no more than hours, minutes out of the water. What about it? She had seen the old men work? Would she stay and see the young men play?

She had stayed, and that had been the start of it. They had gone to a shack at the edge of the village. The food was hot and plentiful, the wine flowed all night long. René had arm-wrestled an immense sailor with a strange name who spoke no English. There had been an argument over a trifling sum of money. A fight had broken out, and René had beaten the foreign sailor first to his knees, then stretched him on the floor, laughing, whooping, shouting as blood ran down his own face and into his open mouth from a cut above his eye.

Madeline had been horrified. And fascinated. She went home very late and sat up half the night writing her story, which turned out to be no kind of newspaper piece at all but a sensual fantasy in which fact and impression were woven together into a fabric more suitable to a romantic novel than to a newspaper feature.

She was still writing when her father staggered into the house at six and almost fell down on the sofa across from her. Really, Daddy. What will mother say? Henry had looked at her as if she'd lost her mind. I have to go back in an hour or so. It's still insanity down at the paper. Isn't it always, Madeline had said with a secret smile, wondering what he might think of her evening in Delacroix. God almighty, he said. Everybody else in the country half crazy, and you act as if nothing has happened. Something is always happening, she told him. What of it? No, he said very softly, his eyes hollow, dark, as if somehow he was looking back into the past. No, nothing like this... Not here, not in America. Not since that September in 1935 when they killed Huey. Listen...

And that was how Madeline had learned that the President of the United States had been assassinated in Dallas while she rode in a shrimp boat on the bright smooth water on a sun-drenched chilly day, and afterward had spent the long evening in a Louisiana French fishing village where no one listened to the radio and no one knew or especially cared. Then or later.

After that, she had gone back to Delacroix many times, time after time. In all that time, he made no move toward intimacy—nothing more than a casual, almost friendly, kiss on the cheek. I think it maddened her a little. I was almost sure that she made every effort to suggest to her friends without actually saying so that she was sexually experienced, that sex, after all, was a form of amusement. Like tennis, except, of course, there's no net. Of course. But it wasn't true. When the strange dalliance with René had begun that November night, she was still a virgin because her desire, for all its heat and depth, was hedged with questions of taste, questions of ... quality. When it happened for the first time, it had to be right. And just then, Madeline hadn't the least idea of what right might mean. She didn't even know what she wanted from René. A brief affair by way of shedding her virtue? Something longer, more complicated? Did she even think of marriage then? The pages of the diary were filled with impressions, waves of feeling, fear and warmth. But nothing concrete. As if the last thing of all things she wanted was to think about what there was or might be or even should be between them.

Then her hand had been forced, you might say. In a way. Henry and Heloise were invited on a junket to Europe. Almost three weeks touring the continent, finding facts, as they used to say. When Lulu and the help left each evening, the house would be Madeline's until the next morning. What happened there would be as secret as the grave.

She left a call for René at Dorgenois's café and bar, where they had spent that first ferocious evening. Come into town, the message said. I want to see you tonight. That and no more. It was explicit enough. Then she had gone to a small boutique that had just opened in the Carrollton Shopping Center and chosen the gown she would be wearing when it happened for the very first time.

When she opened the door to him, she had been wearing that and nothing else. He had smiled that bright smile of his and said nothing, only carried her silently upstairs where it happened again and again until they both lay exhausted on the soaked sheets of her bed.

After that, the pages overflowed with the two of them. There was almost nothing else. What she thought about him. What she supposed he thought about her. Would he come into New Orleans to stay? What would her father, her mother, say and do when they found out? It was wonderful. It was sweeter, finer, more overpowering than she had ever imagined, and yes, she wanted to marry him. In fact . . .

Then the diary broke off. Some time in February of

1964. For over two months there were no entries, and when finally they took up again, the writing was jagged, irregular, almost illegible. The sentences were short, almost journalistic, and the story they told was astonishing and awful.

She had not told her parents about René, and then, suddenly, she had to. She was pregnant, but she couldn't tell René about it. Of course he wanted to marry her. He had already come into town and spoken to her father. But Henry would not hear him out. René was patient. Henry needed time to get used to the idea, René had said. He would wait until her father was in a better frame of mind and try again. And again after that. She needn't worry. They would be together always. Time was on their side.

But it wasn't. The clock inside told Madeline there was no more time. None at all. Even then, deep in June of 1964 and her four months gone, she realized that time had run out for her. Not that time had run out. That it had run out *for her.*

Oh sweet Christ, Madeline had written, *I can't walk up to the altar of St. Louis Cathedral lumbering like a sow and risk delivering on the steps of the sanctuary like a Paris whore in a hard winter. I can't do that.*

And I won't take one of those goddamned tacky two-year honeymoons in Europe and come back swearing on the ninety-eight wounds of Christ that my baby is a year and more younger than it is. I won't do any of that. I just can't.

And having determined so exhaustively what she could not, would not do, Madeline had narrowed the range of choices as to what she could, would, do down to one thing.

The diary went blank again. Nothing was written, everything was clear.

A month later, the impasse was broken. Henry had

come to see that there was no question at all of controlling Madeline, bending her will to his. She was ruining her life, he had told her. She was killing herself. But there was nothing to be gained by his compounding the foolishness, becoming an accessory to it. He agreed to see René again. Madeline's mother reluctantly drew up an engagement announcement and demanded that her husband give it due prominence in the *Item*. If we must do it, Heloise had said, then do it boldly. After all, Maddy's marrying a man from St. Bernard Parish is really no worse than my marrying one from Caddo Parish, is it? Madeline did not record Henry's reply.

Then the pages of the diary filled with showers, parties, the strange effect René had on Madeline's Uptown friends—especially the women. Her women friends were fascinated by René. Kitten Talbot had compared René to Jon Gilbert. Louise Lafreniere had disagreed. Imagine Ray Danton with bigger shoulders. Charlotte Toledano thought he had that certain quality that made Rod Taylor so exciting. Good God, Madeline had mused, every one of them sees in him whatever they'd love to find in a man. But he's mine, and if they want someone like him, they'll have to sort through all those nasty, smelly little fishing villages on their own.

After the wedding it seemed Madeline and René had been very happy. They had moved into the new house on St. Charles, and he began taking courses in business and business law at night even as he was working all day for a drilling company out in Metairie. He learned very rapidly. He was doing very well. In less than three years, with a loan from Madeline, he was working for himself and making excellent money.

Then suddenly the tone of Madeline's diaries changed. Now there was a flavor of cynicism even in the quotations she chose to record. This from Bishop

Talleyrand: "The purpose of language, Monsieur, is to conceal the truth." Had talk come to be so between her and René?

Two things became clear. She could not conceive the child they both wanted. And she did not trust René. Perhaps she never had. When he was away from her for more than an hour or so, she came to suspect that he was betraying her. He enjoyed the company of her women friends too much. It seemed to her that he even preferred talking to her maid Maria more than being with her.

They had begun to have terrible quarrels. René had laughed at her suspicions, claiming his work left him no time to play. But Madeline had insisted René agree with her decision to fire Maria. He had told her she was contemptible, but in the end he had accepted her hysterical demand.

Then, almost as suddenly, it seemed she had put aside her distrust. The diaries became quiet again, filled with bits of poetry, quotations of one kind or another, even recollections of dreams—though none wonderful and Freudian and direct.

My growing up was in those pages alongside René's success in the oil business. I watched seasons and years passing for us all, each one little different from what had gone before. A chill winter, a lovely spring. The Comus Ball, a garden party out in Old Metairie. It was as if Madeline's life had been transformed into a tableaux, a dreamlike ritual movement from one stylized stage set to the next, and, in the round of the year, back over them all once more, and again and again.

My God, I asked myself, is that what our lives are like here? Do we live cycle after cycle without expectation, without regret? Surely not. Surely . . . not.

At last I reached the final volume. Nothing that I had

read so far evoked more than the elements of a marriage that had been much like other marriages—not the best of its kind but surely not the worst. Perhaps René had had other women, perhaps not. If Madeline had strayed, she had not written of it. I suspected there had been nothing to write about.

I set the diary down on the library table as I stood up and stretched. My watch read 2:27 A.M. I felt a little light-headed and walked back to the kitchen to brew coffee. I had spent the last eight hours tracing Madeline's life insofar as she had chosen to present it. And yet I wondered if I knew or understood her any better than before. If someone had asked me to sum up what I knew about her now, I would have said the meeting with René had determined the balance of her life. If she loved or was concerned about anyone else more than in passing, she hadn't written about it.

The coffee helped. There was only that final volume to go. I was very tired, but, having stayed so long with Madeline that night, I decided that I should read it through looking for any changes in her routine. I was sure to be exhausted in the morning, and I was going to sleep in. But Maitland wouldn't care. If his delicately balanced probing of the electorate were done and he was ready to go forward, I'd have heard from him. I smiled, thinking to myself that, when at last he'd finished his private opinion poll, he'd move to have René indicted. It would be more popular than not, and at the very least it would take Henry Holman and the *Item* off his back.

New Orleans is spiritually a very small town, I heard myself saying to myself as I drank down the last of my coffee. And in very small towns, no one is going to defend a man who has killed his wife in cold blood. Because there are too many husbands poised at the very edge of such a thing, too many wives who see rage and alienation in their husbands' eyes across the breakfast table when they glance up from the paper suddenly. It wouldn't do to announce that the logical result of the Great Disillusionment is, after all, only a misdemeanor. They are going to indict René St. Juste and try him and convict him. Unless. Unless...

I went back to the library. The last volume of the diary was lying as I had left it, the cover open, the end papers exposed. I saw a little smudge on the inside cover, but I paid it no mind. It was too late, and I was very tired. I began reading in January of this year.

The surprise, when it came, arrived in slow motion. The language as well as the handwriting was certainly Madeline's. No question at all about that. But something had surely changed. In all the other volumes, there had been a certain luxuriance of tempo to the entries.

No more. Not in that final volume. Almost every entry had a clipped, precise quality—the style of a short news story as opposed to the leisurely style of feature-writing that had characterized all the years before. Almost every entry mentioned the weather, some bit of news she had seen in the paper, an insignificant television program I wouldn't have supposed Madeline would watch, some purchase of clothing or furniture that would never have been mentioned in the earlier volumes. It was as if she had stopped reading, stopped thinking or feeling—as if she had become a recording device to set down the countless trivialities that make up most of our days.

Except in one regard. From the opening pages forward, I could sense a light but increasing drumbeat of tension rising once more between her and René. At first no more than a passing remark, some slight or imagined slight from him. His new habit of spending Friday and part of Saturday in Lafayette. His growing ill-temper as the oil business began sliding inexorably toward the abyss.

Another quarrel tonight. Each of us threatening, each of us finding new ways to strike at one another. I at his original poverty, his dependence on me and my family—even at his manhood. He at my baseless arrogance, my pathetic claim to status in a society that he says has been an absurdity since 1862. God, why did I marry a man from the parishes, a barbarian from a fishing village as far removed from my world as if he had come from the wretched poverty-ridden coast of Normandy?

At last, running quarrels that extended over days and even weeks. Then a bare insinuation that some word or look of René's had frightened her, that for just a moment in the midst of their recriminations, she had thought he was going to strike her.

Again, later, much the same—but stronger. In the midst of a drunken tirade over the collapse of the oil market and the loss of his own self-esteem, he had taken hold of her, shaken her. He had told her that his family was of that same revolutionary blood as St. Juste, the partner and collaborator of Robespierre. His eyes had been bloodshot, saliva dripping from his lips. And do you know what St. Juste said as he himself was pushed under the blade to which he had sent so many, René had shouted at her. He said, We were . . . too merciful, and the knife fell.

He would not make that mistake, should the moment come, René had told her softly as he pushed her from him, let her fall to the floor.

Near the end, Madeline had become certain that René was seeing another woman. Perhaps some street-walker from Decatur Street in the Quarter. That would suit him now, she wrote. Perhaps he could find some sort of pleasure, security, with a whore.

Then in the final entry, it was obvious that she had somehow found out otherwise. She would never have believed who the woman was that René had taken up with. How could he?

There was nothing for it but to end this farce, Madeline had written on that last page. She would confront René, tell him what she knew, and demand a divorce. He would walk away with what was left of his business. Her separate property would be hers. Even before the divorce was filed, she would change her will and find other heirs. René would never see another cent of Holman money.

I let the diary fall closed and stared past the soft light of the lamp on the library table. Outside, I could barely see the trees writhing in the wind, hear the tattoo of rain against the windows.

I felt myself uneasy, frowning. Something was wrong in all this. In those last entries of Madeline's diary, something was missing. There was no analysis of what had happened, no report of how she had felt when he was gone, or how she wondered what might come of it all—not even a mention of the woman's name whom she suspected. It wasn't Madeline. Even in anxiety and despair, she had always been exquisitely conscious, inordinately fond of her own responses, the sheerest fabric of her feelings. Why had she suddenly turned from such introspection to a kind of writing more suited to police reports?

I turned through the pages of the last volume checking an entry here and there along the way. They were much the same—all perfectly coherent, but without the strong undertone of Madeline's emotion.

Until that last entry written the day or night before

Madeline was killed. Only in that one did her feelings seem to emerge—and even then they were muted, stated flatly as if their appearance was their substance, as if Madeline had been a rather disinterested observer instead of a central actor in this drama of a dying marriage.

I let the book fall back as it had been when I began reading it. By then it was just past four, and I knew I shouldn't pour that last brandy. But I did anyhow. It had been a long wretched night in which I had learned a great deal—and nothing at all.

I blinked my eyes, trying to clear my mind to think once more before bed. Then I noticed that the book before me had fallen open to the front endpapers. I had been staring unfocused at the smudge in the upper left-hand corner of the inside cover. I tried to make out if something had been written there, but the light was wrong and the apparent lines wouldn't resolve themselves.

I turned off the library lamp and carried the diary upstairs to my bedroom. In a drawer of my desk, there was an old engineer's pocket sharpener that I had carried to point the drafting pencils I'd used all through law school—the sole useful remnant of a brief romance with a mechanical engineer. I dusted some of the powdered graphite over the smudged area inside the diary cover and squinted at it under my high-intensity desk lamp.

Then it was clear enough. It was just a price marking that someone had erased. It said $4.95. I shrugged and closed the diary, letting it fall on the desk. I undressed slowly, trying to decide whether in my present state it was even safe to attempt a shower. Yes, I thought, you'll sleep better. Ho, I answered myself, as if I'll have any problem sleeping.

I had turned on the shower and was about to step into the rich warm steam when I found myself running out of the bathroom to open the diary and stare at that smudge again. Good God, I thought, you can't buy a leather-bound diary for $4.95.

CHAPTER
14

I felt as if I'd aged twenty years overnight when I finally awakened, but I was at the Uptown Stationers an hour or so after they opened. I'd called a number of other places about the kind of diary Madeline had used, and all of them had directed me to Uptown. No one else regularly stocked personal diaries bound in leather. Of course, I thought. Who but Uptown people would have any use for such things?

A clerk at the stationery counter directed me to a well-dressed older woman in the back where they stocked expensive attaché cases and notebooks.

—Mrs. Frye? I asked.

She looked up, smiled. She was an attractive woman, her thinness partially concealed by her tailored, long-sleeved shirtdress. She wore a gold brooch and earrings, and her hair was carefully tinted and set. I wondered if she were the widow of some reasonably well-off lawyer or doctor who'd waited a bit too long to make his life insurance plans.

—Yes. What can I help you with?

I set Madeline's diary down on her desk. —Is it possible that you sold this book?

She studied it carefully, then looked back up at me, her eyes veiled.

—May I ask how you came by this, Miss?

I reached for my Orleans Parish district attorney's I.D. and showed it to her. —This is official business, I told her.

She looked at the I.D., then back up at me. —I see, she said quietly. —I should have recognized you, Miss Lemoyne. I knew your grandfather. We did his stationery after he retired.

—I remember it. Very thick, creamy. I used to do paper cutouts with the second sheets.

Mrs. Frye smiled. —No one uses anything quite so elegant nowadays. I was sorry to hear of his . . .

—Thank you, I said. —About the diary. It belonged to Madeline St. Juste. Would you know if you'd sold it to her?

—Of course. We've had the line since just after the war. No one else in town carries anything like it, and Mrs. St. Juste bought one from us every year. For years.

I opened the front cover and pointed to the smudge.

—Is that a price? I asked.

Mrs. Frye stared at it for a moment. —Yes, that would be the price.

—I can't believe you sell leather-bound books for $4.95.

—Ordinarily, we don't.

—But then . . .

—You see, it's dated merchandise. Its value to a customer declines from the beginning of the year until . . .

—Then this diary was bought . . . on sale?

202 A CIVIL DEATH

—Yes. It would have been sold in late September.

—September? How can you be sure?

—Because in our Fall Shoppers Sale dated merchandise is marked off ninety percent. The diary sold originally for $49.95. Since it's marked $4.95 . . .

—Is there any chance that this book was wrongly marked?

—No, Mrs. Frye said. —None at all. We don't pencil price markings on any of our better merchandise . . . until it goes on sale.

I was more than surprised. I couldn't quite focus my mind on what I'd found out, on what it might mean.

—Anyhow, Mrs. Frye went on, —I remember selling this book to Mrs. St. Juste a little over a month ago. She'd bought one as usual at the end of last year. But something happened to it.

—Did she say what?

—Only that it had been ruined, utterly ruined. I had the notion that she'd spilled something on it. She was lucky. We had only one or two left in September.

—But all the pages of this book are full from January until the day before her death.

—Perhaps she copied the pages of the spoiled book into the new one.

I walked out of the shop in a daze. Mrs. Frye said she'd see if she could locate copies of the sales slips for the two diaries, the one Madeline had bought in December of last year—and the replacement she'd bought in September. I might need the slips. As exculpatory evidence.

I drove into Audubon Park and stopped the car under one of the old live oaks. Like magnolias, they keep their leaves in winter, and each giant tree was a peaceful moment of green in the gray-brown expanse of blighted grass, shrubs, and leafless trees.

Another look through those diary pages told me my first impression had been right. Most of the entries didn't ring true. They were carefully written to detail a scenario Madeline wanted others to believe had taken place between her and René. I was sure they hadn't been written from the experience of the moment, and I suspected that nothing had happened to the original diary at all. But how could I possibly prove what my intuition told me?

As I started the car up again and headed downtown along Magazine, I thought absently of Mrs. Frye talking about my grandfather's stationery. Then it struck me, and I skidded the car to a stop at the curb and ran through the pages of the diary again looking for what I knew I wouldn't find.

There was no mention of my grandfather's death or that of my father just after. Even more obvious, there was no mention of Madeline's mother's death at all. Three deaths of people close to her in three months, and not a word about them in the pages of her diary.

Because, of course, this last volume was no diary at all.

It was a carefully planned and executed document with a single purpose, and the purpose was obvious once you realized that all the entries had been written in a relatively short time, once you knew what to look for.

Madeline St. Juste had intended for her last diary, which had been left open on the secretary desk in her bedroom, to be read. The entries had been fabricated to show René's growing alienation, his despair over his financial situation, and Madeline's increasing fear of him. Madeline had set her husband up. For a charge of murder.

It had been cleverly done, and if I hadn't taken all the

diaries home and read them through—or if I had not known Madeline as well as I did—I might never have noticed.

But why? Had she goaded René into killing her, leaving behind the diary as additional evidence to drive home the obvious? That seemed absurd. What if René had simply chosen to walk away and file for divorce, saying, at last, the hell with the money? After all, I thought, you can't require someone to murder you on schedule.

It didn't work. But there had to be an explanation, and the whole equation had shifted. Madeline wasn't just a victim any longer. Whatever had happened, however it had happened, she had been consciously involved in her own death. That much I was sure of.

I turned at Valence Street and headed back Uptown on St. Charles. It was almost midday. I didn't know whether Lulu Washington would still be working at the St. Juste house or not, but I decided to try it before I drove out to Mid-City. It was time for me to talk to her again.

For a moment I thought of stopping at a drugstore and calling Rat Trapp. Then I decided against it. Rat's head-on interrogation methods wouldn't budge Lulu. Whatever she might be hiding must be far more painful than anything Rat could threaten her with. If I was going to find out the truth, I'd have to be very indirect. So I'd better do it on my own.

I parked at curbside and walked up to the St. Juste front door, but there was no answer when I rang the chimes. After another try, I followed the driveway around the side of the house to the rear. From there, I could look into the kitchen and breakfast room through large windows that opened out on the bushes and evergreens planted thick around the borders of the bricked courtyard.

Lulu sat at the breakfast-room table, her hands folded, her eyes open, staring ahead as if she had been hypnotized by someone long ago and the command to awaken had never been given. I leaned across the camellia bushes and tapped on the window nearest her. After a moment, she looked over at me with no sign of recognition in her eyes—or perhaps as if she saw in me someone to fear, someone bearing more awful news— beyond what she could bear.

Lulu shuffled to the back door and let me into the kitchen. It seemed to me that she had aged even since I had last seen her.

—Mr. St. Juste's not here, she said softly. —That's how come I don't answer the door. No need. Nobody want to see me.

—I do, I told her. —I came to see you. I wasn't sure you'd be here since they charged Mr. St. Juste...

Lulu's expression darkened. She became alert, close to suspicious. —Working here is all I know. I ain't no judge. I leave that to folks who find out the truth. What you want to talk to me for, honey?

I tried to think how I could calm Lulu, get her started talking on the part of Madeline's past I was sure only she could reveal. —I don't want to talk about her death right now. I want to talk about... the beginning.

—Huh?

—I want to know what happened back in 1963, when Madeline first met René, when they were going together.

That expression of fear came back into her eyes. Sun had broken through the clouds for a moment. The kitchen had windows on two sides and now the interior was ablaze with soft autumn sunlight.

—Why you want to know about that? I mean, that's done and gone.

—Lulu, I know that before they were married, Miss Madeline had an abortion.

Lulu's lips sealed themselves as if she meant never to talk again. I waited. Sooner or later she'd tell me. If I was right, she'd tell me everything I wanted to know because she couldn't help the telling, had been wanting to tell and be released from it at least since that Friday night and Saturday morning—if not for years before.

—Where you get that notion?

I held up the last volume of the diary. Lulu started to reach out for it.

—You been reading my baby's private books?

—Every page of every volume, I said. —From before I was born until... You helped her, didn't you? In 1964, a woman didn't walk into a clinic and tell the doctor she had a problem. Later it would be that way, but not yet, not then.

Lulu nodded, tears beginning to flow down her wrinkled cheeks. —She come to me, say, "Momma, I can't go in front of all them people I known all my life looking like I'm carrying. I just can't."

—So you...helped.

—I didn't do nothing right off. I try to talk to her. I say, "Baby, it don't matter. Child come into the world, that's a celebration, hear?" But she didn't pay no mind. Just cry and cry. Then I tell her to run off, say her daddy pushed her to it. Come back in a year or so. She say, "Don't tell me that, Momma. René wants us to live in New Orleans."

It was like listening to those pages of Madeline's diary coming to life in Lulu's voice. She was the one

who had tried the other side of the case, the one
against whom Madeline had directed her arguments.

—So then...

Lulu nodded slowly. Now the tears were running
freely. I reached over and took her hand. There was no
strength in it. She was mourning, and nothing I could
say or do would make it better.

—I killed both of 'em, she said, her voice choking.
—I took her to that old woman on Esplanade, and that
did for the poor baby.

—Both of them?

—The other one was her...

—What are you saying, I almost shouted, both be-
lieving and unable to believe what I thought I was
hearing. —You didn't shoot Madeline. You couldn't...

—I just as well have, Lulu went on, not even noticing me then, so deep was her sorrow. —I just as well
gone in and threw down on her and pulled that trigger.

—Tell me what you mean, I said, my voice returning
to normal.

—That woman out on Esplanade ruined her. Old fool
ruined my little girl.

—The abortion...

—Child that old woman took from her was the last
one she could get. I don't know. Something got tore,
scarred. Lord God, afterward we went everywhere to
see about it. We went way up north to some place in
Minnesota. We went over to Texas. New York one
winter just before it come Christmas... always saying
to Mr. René and her daddy it was something else,
somewhere else. Just the two of us, 'cause she was
crazy he'd find out.

—René didn't know?

Lulu shook her head furiously, voice lowered to a
conspiratorial whisper. —Uh-uh. Not ever. He don't

know till this day. See, he come from them Cajun Catholics, Miss Denise. He wouldn't of cared if my little girl come waddling up the church aisle like a cow fixing to throw a calf. What do he care? A fine son, a pretty daughter... And he be right, too...

He wouldn't have cared, I thought. Not then, not ever. He would have seen the child as... a celebration, and laughed to know that he would be a father almost as soon as he became a husband.

Lulu was watching me. She knew what I was thinking.

—No use to talk, Miss Denise. You can say right or wrong, but *she* had to do it. Come time after, she had to live with it...

—All those years...

—Every day of all them years, day after day, year after year. What we done wasn't never out of our minds. Then one day last September...

—September, I repeated.

—She come home from somewhere, walk in here whilst I'm working, and she say, "He's got another woman, Momma. I'm going to lose him. And if I lose him, I've lost everything. My life not worth nothing." I say, "Put it out of mind, sugar. He gonna tire hisself out and come on back home. You see. They all do it, and they all come trucking back home when they done their dirt."

—She told you about Elena Quintero?

—She don't say who, just what. Woman don't need much to be happy. She think she do, but she don't. But what she need she got to have. She couldn't leave it be. She kept on after it, till...

—What? I asked.

Lulu fell silent. But we were to the point where personal history became case history. I had to stretch what I knew by stating what I suspected as absolute truth.

—I read her diary, Lulu. Madeline . . . planned her death, didn't she? Like a play. Just tell me your role in it.

When Lulu lifted her tear-filled eyes from the kitchen tabletop to meet mine, I knew my gamble had paid off.

—One day she tell me, "Momma, I want it over, done with." I say, "Honey, that not for you or me to say. When it's enough, we be took from here up to Glory."

Madeline had laughed at that, Lulu told me. There was going to be no glory for her. By then Madeline had come to believe in nothing transcendent, nothing holy or splendid beyond the anguish of the world—except that perhaps in some indistinct kind of hell, she would have to face the child she had destroyed in the name of Uptown propriety. Then she had told Lulu what she wanted.

—She say, "You got to help me. You got to help me the only way left for you to." Then she tell me what she gonna do.

She was going to kill herself. At first Lulu had thought she was simply upset and a little rest, a drink, would bring her around. But soon she realized that Madeline had laid out her plan so fully, so carefully, that there could be no doubt at all that she meant what she was saying.

It was to be done so as to make very sure that René St. Juste would be blamed for it. The bits of evidence would be arranged in such a way as to lead any reasonably competent detective to René in a matter of hours —days at the most.

—No, I told her, Lulu said. —I done whatever you

asked since you was a little girl. But you can't ask me to...

—Oh my God, she wanted you to...

—No, not that. She knew not to ask that. She'd do it herself. She gonna dress up in her new gown and robe with her hair fixed the day before. She gonna wear one of them rubber kitchen gloves on her hand. Then when it was done, I suppose to take off the glove, put it in a bag with the gun and all the jewelry, and go on home. And wait...

I closed my eyes, seeing Madeline's face in my imagination, her mouth twisted, eyes crazed. Madeline had broken the glass in the French door to the study, taken the pistol from the gun rack.

Then one thing more struck me, and I felt myself sick, hollow. I had been part of her plan, too. Madeline had called me, insisted I come for brunch intending that I should find her body, should draw the conclusions her fabricated evidence would force me to—and lead the pack after René until he was convicted of a crime his supposed victim actually had committed.

—But you wouldn't do it? I said. —Is that what you're telling me?

Lulu nodded slowly. —I talk to her all day Friday. It start in the morning and go on hour after hour. Lord God, I follow her around the house saying how it's wrong, how it don't make no sense even if that fool man don't come home. I say how she's a fine-looking woman with money of her own. She can pick any life she want. She say, "I already picked, Momma. I picked years ago when I made you take me to that old woman out on Esplanade Avenue. Only I didn't know it then. All I was thinking was what Uptown folks was gonna say, how I'd feel. But I picked then. I picked death."

—But you didn't leave her like that.

—About five o'clock or so, she seem to come around. She say she gonna think it over some more, talk to Mr. St. Juste one more time, see they can't get things back together. I say, All right. But I gonna stay with you. I don't like that talk. "No," she say, "I need to think all by myself. I call you later at home."

—You believed her?

Lulu drew a deep breath and looked down at the table.

—I don't know, she said slowly. —Right now, sitting here talking to you, I don't know. I was so tired. Things been wrong in this house for so long. Say I wanted to believe it. Say it wasn't no way I could stay with her, seeing to her all day and all night every day and night whether I believed it or not. So I put them kitchen gloves in my purse and took 'em with me just like that was gonna keep her from... Then I kissed her and told her goodbye, I'd call after a while.

—Did you?

—Oh yes. I call, but the line was busy.

—Madeline phoned me that night.

—Maybe it was you. Maybe somebody else. I call two, three times. She talking, so I think, it's all right. She got one of her lady friends on the phone going on about how bad things was. Long as she's talking...

—Then you didn't know anything more until you heard the news the next day?

Lulu looked up at me, eyes dry then as if she had cried all the tears she had to cry. —No, I knew.

—You went back?

—I didn't need to. After midnight, I called once more. Let it ring for fifteen, twenty minutes. And when it went on ringing and no answer, I knew.

—You couldn't know. Madeline could have put the phone under a pillow. She could have gone out. She could have been drinking and fallen asleep.

—I knew, Lulu repeated, nodding to herself. —I went to mourning right then, 'cause I knew. Wasn't any of them things you say. She was gone. And then there it was on the TV news and you come by, and sure enough . . .

We sat silent for a while. It was almost all there. A scarlet thread running backward to a time before I could remember. A choice made by a woman I had thought I knew as well as anyone, but who was a dark stranger I had never met. Guilt, sorrow, pride of place, a marriage ruined by a single choice that had been made before the marriage even began—all of it channeled inexorably down to one final evening and the events that had taken place after Lulu left the St. Juste house.

—So you didn't take the jewelry, did you?

—No ma'am. It was like with the gloves. I reckon if I take the gloves and leave the jewelry all there, then she can't . . . But she did. Some way or other, she did.

No, I thought. She didn't—at least not by herself. She couldn't have. Not because of the missing jewelry. That could be anywhere—perhaps planted like the earring so that, if discovered, it would point once more to René. But what about the gun? Where could the gun have gone? And if Lulu was telling me the truth, who had carried it away?

—Why didn't you tell me, Lulu? I asked her. I felt as tired as she must be, but I was too close to some kind of truth to stop then. —Why didn't you tell me when I came to your house?

Lulu's head came up. Her expression was implacable.

—'Cause it was what she wanted. Keeping out of it, staying quiet... That was the last thing I could do for her.

—But don't you see the pain you've caused Mr. St. Juste? Elena Quintero?

Lulu's eyes glittered. Her mouth was like a lipless slash across her face.

—I don't owe that man nothing. My little girl calling out to him for help over the years and he don't hear, he don't care...and that woman...a common street whore...

She wasn't going to be moved and it didn't matter. It wasn't my job to try to convince Lulu Washington that she had done wrong. She had spent most of her life taking care of Madeline, sharing her happiness, living her pain. If she could not dissuade Madeline from her terrible plan, she could stand mute and let that plan unfold, no matter what the consequences. She could let Madeline end the pain that had gone on so long. That was all Lulu had left to hold on to. Still, there was one more question I had to ask.

—Why just then? Why did Miss Madeline decide to do... what she did on that certain Friday night?

—I don't know that, Lulu said, shaking her head. —I guess it wasn't any hope left, and she was tired. If I knew why, maybe I could of...

—I don't think so, I said. —I think it was... always going to happen.

—See, Lulu crooned, her voice soft and distant, —I killed 'em both, that poor baby that never saw the light twenty-four years ago, and my little girl, too.

The sun had vanished once more, swallowed up by dark clouds, and a light misty rain was falling. I stood up and walked to the phone then. It was time to call Rat Trapp and introduce him to history.

CHAPTER

15

When I called Rat, he came out to the St. Juste house quickly. I met him at the front door, led him into the library, and told him about the diaries—especially about that extra diary Madeline had bought and filled in to suit her purposes. He looked at it and shook his head.

—Sonofabitch, I had care, control, and custody of them damned things and I never...

—You didn't know her. I did. When I read all of them, and then hit this last one...

Rat smiled and patted my hand. —I'm not gonna say you're a natural, 'cause you've only done it this once so far, but you sure as hell have gone and done it.

—Now go in the kitchen and talk to Lulu Washington.

—She got something to tell me?

—Oh yes, I said wearily. —Yes, I believe she does.

Rat went back into the kitchen and sat down with some fresh coffee Lulu had brewed. Then he listened to it all from the beginning as she told her story in a flat monotonous voice that was harsh and worn thin by weariness and repetition.

I couldn't go through it all again, so I sat in the library drinking some of René's whiskey, remembering. Madeline had been afraid of this place, of the people, of the long, demanding, desolate past that dictated to all of us who chose to live out our lives Uptown. She made one desperate attempt to find her way back to the living, then ruined that before it could come to anything. Then it struck me: Was I thinking of Madeline's past or my future?

I wiped tears off my face when Rat came quietly back into the room. I was ashamed of the self-pity mixed with mourning anew for Madeline. Poor little girls, never happy. Rat took my hand.

—I understand, girl. I truly do. But this is gonna have to wait.

—It can't wait. I have to get out of here, out of this damned city.

—Don't be foolish. Maybe you got to get out of yourself, walk away from who you've been. I don't know. But first we got to drive a good old woman home to her sister's place. Then we got to figure out what happened. What really, honest to God happened.

Rat was right. The first thing was to drive Lulu home. That part we managed quickly. The ceaseless rain was falling hard again when we pulled up in front of the neat old-fashioned house in Mid-City. Rat handed me his yellow police poncho, and I walked Lulu up to the door, both of us covered against the rain.

—I'm glad it's so near finished, she told me as we stood on the porch. —Oh, Lord, to be done with it . . . to put it behind me and walk on.

—I think it's done as far as you're concerned, Lulu, I said, kissing her. —Try to put it out of mind.

She looked up at me in surprise as she opened the door with her key.

—I'm not talking about Miss Madeline, she said in a strong certain voice, as if perhaps she had made a decision of her own. —I'm talking about living.

The door closed behind her before I could say anything. I had only time to think, Another casualty, as I walked back to Rat's car.

—Do you buy it? I asked as he pulled away.

—Lulu's story? Shit yes. Don't you?

—Of course. But I thought a Gonzo detective . . .

—Oh, dear one, wake up and open those lovely eyes. Gonzo looks for stories like that. Your basic Gonzo wants something so weird, so human he can believe it.

—Oh . . .

—So all we got left to do now is what the fuck we started out having to do. Reckon on who shot her.

—What if there actually *was* a break-in? The burglar found Madeline dead. He took the jewelry, took the gun . . .

Rat laughed so loudly and suddenly that we almost ran into the curb.

—Oh shit, baby. You got to make it up with Wes. Youall could write mystery novels together.

—No?

—Honey, a ordinary burglar come in and see that woman cooled, he'd do track speed getting out of there. How about we're still doing Renny-baby?

—Rat, when will you let go and . . .

—When I'm satisfied, woman. You hear? When I'm satisfied. How come you say he couldn't have come home right in the middle of all that shit, after Lulu

went home and Madeline's plan looks like down the
drain. And he's tanked, and they fight, and he blows
her away and makes her little playacting plan come to
life. See, he does just what it was she wanted to make
it *look* like he did. And maybe he even *knows* that.
Maybe he knows everything we know, and that means
he's standing pat 'cause sooner or later somebody was
gonna crack Lulu Washington wide open, and . . .

—Hold up, I almost shouted at him. —Don't tell me
that. Were you going after Lulu again?

—Well . . .

—No, because the diaries were the key to it—all of
them. I wouldn't have gone back to Lulu if it hadn't
been for reading them, and René couldn't possibly
count on that.

Rat said nothing as we drove down North Carrollton.
His silence was a kind of reward. If I had cared any
longer about my work, it would have made me feel
very good indeed.

But I didn't. I wasn't even thinking of my work. Is it
too much to say that I hardly cared any longer about
the details of Madeline's dying? I was thinking about
my life.

I was thinking how, if I still had the chance, I'd never
fail it as Madeline had. If I had let myself get pregnant
by Wesley Colvin, I'd hire the Olympia Brass Band and
march up Bourbon Street announcing it to the world
and handing out wedding invitations—for a week after
my *accouchement*. But I was wondering if I'd already let
that chance go by.

—Rat, have you seen Wes?

—Oh, sure. We had us a steak at Charlie's last night.
Then we went out to the Kit-Kat Klub and drank whiskey and talked dirty.

—I'll bet you did. How . . . is he?

—How is he? My boy Wes? Why honey, he's fine. I mean, that man's on a roll...

—I'm glad.

—He's so goddamned fine he drank himself sick and got to whining like a ninny about one-thirty last night, and I had to roll his ass home and put him to bed.

—Why...?

—What the fuck you think, girl? Dumb bastard is a one-woman man. I'm telling him how good he done on the Quintero connection, and he's telling me it cost him the rest of his life, and he wishes the goddamn pictures and the story was all shoved up the fat man's ass— meaning Henry Holman's—and he was back in the sack with you. That's how fine he is.

—It was a cheap sensationalist trick, I said, my anger not quite spent. —It hurt people. If Paul Quintero comes to...

Rat shrugged, his eyes straight ahead. —You can quit beating Wesley on the head about that. Paul Quintero died a couple of hours ago at Touro Infirmary. His loving wife was right there by his side, the way it's supposed to be.

I leaned back and closed my eyes. It had to be for the best. For a long time now I have needed to believe that the dead suffer no pain at all. Because pain is what keeps insisting that we are alive.

—Wes said he'd call you, but it wouldn't do no good...

—Yes it would, I said quickly, before Rat could finish.

—You reckon?

—I... reckon. I... never asked him... to be perfect, I heard myself saying. As if I were desperate to be with my cheap sensationalist redneck once more.

—Well good. 'Cause he's not going to be. Now or later. You want me to carry you on by his place?

I almost said yes, but there was something else that had to be done. Not my work. Something far more important. A duty, a family duty. No one could do it but me, and it had to be done right then. It just had to.

—No. Drop me by Henry Holman's, I told Rat.

—You sure? It's near quitting time, and Wes is gonna get tanked again if you don't . . .

—Listen, call Wes. Tell him I've gone to Henry's. Henry has to know the truth, and he has to hear it from me—not from some stranger, not from a story in his own paper. Tell Wes I'll see him when that's done.

—I can do that, Rat said, smiling. —You gonna go home after?

—My car's in front of the St. Juste house. I'll pick it up and drive to Wes's.

—Ah, Rat said, the smile growing wider. —You know, that's nice.

—What?

—You bringing this whole business up. I mean about you and Wes. See, I was supposed to bring it up myself, 'cause he said if I was any kind of friend, I wasn't gonna let his life get ruined without taking my best shot.

We talked and laughed together for the block or two remaining before Rat pulled up in front of Henry's house on St. Charles. I leaned over and kissed him.

—It's good that Wes and I have a friend like you, I told him.

—Listen, girl, I wouldn't give youall away cheap, neither. We've been through a lot together.

—With a lot more to go, I added.

—Take the poncho and stay dry, he said. —I'll pick it up over at Wes's.

—Not tonight, I told him.

—Oh, no, sweet one. Never tonight.

Rat waited until I had rung Henry's bell. As Henry opened the door, I heard him pulling away.

Henry had been drinking. I expected that. But he wasn't drunk. He stared at me for a moment as if he were trying to recognize someone he hadn't seen in a long time.

—May I come in? I asked.

—Dennie? Sure you can. It's cold and wet out there. They said on the news it could snow.

—They always say that, don't they?

—Well, but it never happens, does it?

—Are you still angry with me, Uncle Henry?

He frowned as if he could imagine no reason in the world that we might have quarreled. Then it came to him.

—Oh, that bail business. Did I say something awful, honey? You know I didn't mean it. You're as precious to me as . . .

—As Madeline?

—Yes, he said somberly. —As Madeline.

We walked back to his study where a warm fire burned in the grate. There was a bottle of Jack Daniel's Black Label almost empty on an end table beside his chair.

—You want a little of this, or maybe a glass of wine, honey?

—That will be just fine. I'll find a glass. You sit down and watch the fire.

I managed to find my way through the shadows to the bar. I filled my glass half full of club soda. I had learned something about drinking with rednecks. You must protect yourself before the fact, not after. They drink deep and intensely. It is a form of communication between them. What I had to tell Henry demanded communication.

I sat down in a chair across from his, held out my glass, and let him fill it.

—I have a thing to tell you, I began.

He heard me through to the end. Not, God knows, because he wanted to, but because he had to. Because in the desolation of his loss, with nothing but those crepe myrtle trees far out in his backyard to visit each day in memory of her, even the opening of a secret life she had lived that he had never known, never guessed at, was something he could not ignore, turn away from. The hunger of the living for the beloved dead can be appalling. No characteristic detail, no telling phrase, no remembered gesture is so insignificant that it does not loom large, a priceless treasure, in the mind and heart of one left behind.

As I spoke, I tried not to look at him, not to meet his eyes, but we had known one another, cared for each other too long for me to stare away from him into the fireplace, at the thick drapes, at the soft light out in the empty foyer.

—Oh God, he breathed when I was done. —And you believe it? All of it?

—Yes, I said in the same quiet voice in which I had told what I had to tell. —I'll bring you the diaries. Lulu will come and . . .

Henry waved his hand as if he were pushing something away. —No, no, he said, his voice close to failing him. —I . . . don't want that. Jesus, I don't want to hear it again.

—I'm sorry, I said futilely. —But you had to know. And I had to tell you.

—You had to tell me, he repeated in agreement, his large head nodding, his thin iron-gray hair glinting in the firelight. He threw down the rest of his whiskey and stared into the fire as I did.

—How could she ever think I'd . . .

I said nothing. I didn't say, Henry, if she'd come to you carrying the child of a man you despised for being what you yourself had been when first you came down to New Orleans from Caddo Parish over fifty years ago, what would you have said? What would you have done? What would you have told her to ease the fear of humiliation among the only kind of people she knew, the only kind of people she would ever know?

—Lord God, Henry said, —if she'd never met that coonass sonofabitch . . .

—If she'd never had a redneck father . . . I shot back at him before I could check myself.

He paused and stared at me, his tired eyes dark and murderous, his face even closer to scarlet than it usually was.

—Go on, he said slowly, accentuating every word. —You can turn it on me, you can blame her poor dead momma. You can sure as hell blame this stinking city I wish to God I've never seen. But the last turn of the screw . . .

—Don't go on like that, Henry, I said. —The first turn of the screw took my godmother out to Esplanade Avenue to a dirty rundown two-story ruin where nice girls canceled silly mistakes.

He shook his head violently, ignoring me. —The last turn of the screw was that bastard playing around with that greaser judge.

—You know who Elena Quintero is?

—Oh hell yes. I've known who she was since Madeline ran her off to keep René from rutting her in the pantry. The kitchen maid who went to law school . . . but never let go her Latin lover. My God, they were

grunting and hunching behind my little girl's back
for . . .

—No, I said.

—No? What the hell do you mean, No? There's no
such thing as negative evidence, is there? She was their
maid. He paid for her schooling, and he's shacking up
with her now. Don't tell me no.

Henry was standing now, his face mottled, twisted
into a mask of hatred and vengefulness.

—One more turn of the screw, he screamed so loudly
that I came up out of my chair and backed away from
him toward the foyer. —And the last turn of the screw
cancels . . . all debts, everything.

He stumbled from the room, still shouting incoher-
ently, and I saw him slip and almost fall as he began to
climb the stairs. I wanted to go and help him to his
bedroom, but something kept me from it. It was as if he
had been transformed, changed from a shrewd, kindly,
lethal old man who, despite his wickedness and icy
self-seeking over fifty years, had always loved me—
into a raving abstract principle of vengeance. I couldn't
go to him. I just couldn't. I heard him above me then,
cursing, insisting, falling silent, then starting to bellow
once more as I walked quickly through the dim foyer,
stepped outside into cold implacable winter rain and
closed the heavy door behind me.

I found my car and got inside. In a few moments, I
could be at Wes's apartment. I still had my key. It was
almost evening, and the dense clouds above had already brought deep twilight to the city streets. The
apartment would be warm, and I could kindle a fire
and wait there thinking of what to say until he came
home from the *Item*. The sound of rain falling on the
car's canvas roof seemed lonelier than ever, and I

wished it were a summer rain and Wes and I were parked on a beach somewhere in the Florida Keys. Or along the Greek coast on the isthmus near Corinth. Anywhere at all but Uptown New Orleans, and me still a servant of the law. Crazy Lady.

Then I saw René St. Juste pull into his circular driveway, get out of his car, and walk slowly up to his front door. He opened it and walked inside. Whether Rat knew it or not, I was certain now that René had not killed Madeline. It would have been too fortuitous for him to step into the middle of the harrowing play she'd created at exactly the right moment, to do exactly what she wanted the town to believe he had done. Neither gods nor machines work so perfectly. If we know anything at all, every one of us has learned that.

I sighed, pulled the yellow poncho Rat had loaned me over my head and stepped out into the rain. I didn't want to go through it all once more, but I owed René at least enough of it to give him the first decent night's sleep he'd had since it began. My God, I thought, I keep tripping across debts I owe. When will I find one I owe myself? The answer came quickly: as soon as I was done here, and could drive the few blocks to Wes's place.

René was surprised to see me.

—An official visit? he asked mildly.

—No . . . and yes. We've found out a lot. I thought you should know.

—That's kind of you, he smiled as he took the poncho and threw it on a chair in the foyer. —I didn't know suspects were kept up to date.

—You're not my suspect anymore, I told him. —You never really were.

—Then you know who . . . ?

—No, damn it. We know everything except that.

May I have a double scotch, René? It's very complicated and very strange.

—It sounds as if I should make one for myself.

—Please do.

He smiled. It was as if that old feeling that had always stirred between us was restored for a moment. Not sexual, not even attraction. Simply communication. I smiled to myself. Do I have a special gift to speak to Cajuns from the marshes and rednecks from the piney woods?

We were back in René's study then. An hour must have passed before I was done. By that time it was dark in the courtyard outside, and the room was lit with the single mellow bulb of a ship's captain's lamp swathed in a tan parchment shade. The wall behind René was taken up with his gun racks, filled with rifles and shotguns, weapons he had collected since he had started to make money, and a few he had brought in from the parish with him.

As I spoke, René sat facing toward the French doors that had been repaired, the new pane bright and unmarked except for a small paper tag that no one had thought to scratch off. When I fell silent at last he turned, and I could see tears running down his cheeks.

—Poor little girl, he said softly, and I felt my breath catch in my throat. —Why would she have...?

—René, I'd rather leave that with you. No, that doesn't sound right. It's left with all of us.

But René wasn't listening, and I could barely hear him as he spoke again.

—We could have had a...grown son. Or a daughter. A few years younger than you, Dennie.

—Yes, I said.

—I did love her. I loved her for years.

—I know...

—But I came to feel like a suitor instead of a husband, a suitor who'd been turned down so often that he finally came to believe it was no use ... because the girl he loves ... has died. In one sense or another.

I nodded, feeling his pain. Not a fresh wound, stabbing to the heart. The pain of an old wound opened once again.

—There are still two questions, I told René. —If Madeline went through with it after Lulu left for home, who took the gun ... and the jewelry?

René shook his head. —It's too bizarre, tóo ... dark. There's no one I know who would have agreed to ... Christ, Dennie, half Madeline's friends are in analysis. If she'd asked one of them, every psychiatrist's phone in town would have been ringing off the hook. We'd have heard.

—We'll find out, I said. —Sooner or later, we'll find out.

—Make it sooner, René said somberly. —If you can.

—Maybe you can answer the other question. I doubt that it really bears on the case, but if I don't find out, it will always ... be there.

—What?

—Why did Madeline choose that certain Friday night of all the awful nights she visited on herself? Why not before? Or later? Madeline had had the idea, she'd bought the new diary and done away with the old one. She'd planned all the details ... but why that night?

René lifted his hand as if to silence me. His face was ashy, aged in the soft yellow light of the single lamp.

—I think I can answer that one, he said slowly, softly. —You'll find out anyhow. Everyone will know, but you'll be the only one who ...

René's voice faded. He cleared his throat and stood up, reaching for my glass and his own.

—That last argument... Friday morning when I told Madeline I wanted a divorce...

—Yes...?

—It was very bad. It went on and on, as if we were doomed to repeat the same accusations over and over. There was no end to it, until I told her... and then it ended, and I walked out of the house.

—Told her...?

—You see, I didn't want to tell her. I didn't want to hurt her. I only wanted free of... I didn't know what it would mean, because I never knew till tonight what she'd done before we were married.

I closed my eyes. If René had vanished at that moment, it wouldn't have mattered. I knew what he was going to say before he said it, and I knew for certain that it had been, indeed, the final turn of the screw.

—Elena's pregnant... with our child. She'll have the baby sometime in March.

—Yes, I said, —that would have...

—If only I'd known, René began. —My God, if only I'd known in... what was it? 1964? Tonight Madeline'd be alive and we'd be together. Our little girl, our son, would be...

Then he wiped his eyes with the back of his hand and shrugged. —But it wasn't going to be that way, was it? It never was going to... Let me freshen these drinks, he said rising to his feet. But the bottle we had been drinking from was empty.

—I'll get some scotch from the library. Or perhaps a glass of champagne. It's worth some kind of a celebration... at least a little one, isn't it? A toast to the dead... and the yet unborn.

—René, it's not over yet, I called out after him as he walked down the hall to the bar in the library.

—Yes, it is, he called back to me. —It is for Elena and

me. What do you say? More scotch, or a glass of champagne? For a new arrival, a child who's been waiting to be born for over twenty years.

I saw the reflection of a light switched on. There was a moment of silence, and then I heard a strange, vicious sound, like a cork popping from a champagne bottle, but joyless, angry, deadly.

—Ah, Christ, I heard René choke out, then glass breaking, and someone falling to the floor.

CHAPTER

16

René...? I called out, but there was no answer. No sound at all.

—René...? I called again, and then stepped into the hallway and started down toward the center of the house. I reached the foyer and looked across it toward the library, which was lighted only by baby spots recessed in the ceiling.

René was lying on the floor near the bar surrounded by broken glass, his head and face covered with blood. I started to run toward him, but as I did, something stirred in the deep shadows at the far end of the library. I saw a splash of light and heard that angry, snarling, popping sound again as a piece of plaster exploded off the wall next to my head. For some fraction of a second, I was transfixed. Someone had come to kill René, and now he had heard me, seen me.

Then I turned and ran back down the dark hallway, hearing as I ran some other sound in the distance—a sound like the door chimes.

I wanted to run into the den, tear open René's gun case, but I knew there was no time. Before I could find cartridges and load anything, it would be too late. I ran until I reached the end of the hall and pushed open a bedroom door. I hurled myself into the dark room, then turned and looked back through the crack of the unclosed door toward the foyer.

The shooter had stepped into the light. He was very tall, dressed in black: black jeans, a black sweater, and one of those ski masks that hides everything but the eyes. I knew he couldn't see me down the dark length of the hallway, but I shrank back as if he had X-ray vision. He had paused for a moment, looking at something. Then he reached over and picked it up from the chair where René had dropped it. It was Rat's yellow poncho, and stenciled on the back in large black letters was NOPD.

Oh God, I thought, he'll think I'm an officer. And even off duty, a policeman carries his gun. He'll either run or come after me slowly. I'll have a chance. If I can get to a phone . . .

I closed the bedroom door softly so that he'd have to check out every room. As I backed away from the door into the utter darkness, I glanced from side to side, trying to make out where furniture was, where the windows were.

Then, suddenly, I realized that I knew exactly where everything was. I was in Madeline's room, with a killer coming down the hallway after me.

For a moment, I lost control. I was Madeline, and there was no hope. But I had changed my mind. I wanted to live. I wanted to forgive René and let him live, too. I thought I was even prepared to forgive myself.

Then I caught hold and picked up the phone on a

bedside table. But when I lifted the receiver to my ear I heard only silence. I tried punching buttons, but the phone was dead. Probably the line had been cut. I turned to the windows, tearing the drapes and curtains aside as quickly and silently as I could. But as I did, as I looked out through the rain-sprinkled windowpanes at the cars passing by on St. Charles Avenue, I saw that there was no exit. I should have realized that from the start. How many times over the years had I seen those burglar bars from the outside?

I ran quietly across the room to the windows that opened onto the side yard. Even if I smashed the glass, there was the familiar pattern of wrought-iron bars on the outside that would keep me from breaking free. Behind me, I could hear the shooter's footsteps, a door opening, a long pause, and a door closing once more. He was working his way down the hall, room by room. He had all the time in the world and a silenced pistol. No one would be coming. No one would hear anything.

And on a tomorrow I would never see, René and I would be found dead together in this house. The questions would begin and never quite be ended. If the shooter were very clever, after he'd killed me he'd take the gun back to the library where René lay dead of a head wound. He'd put the gun in René's hand, and vanish.

It wouldn't work for Rat. I could not say whether Wes would believe it. But it would have the bare shabby appearance of a murder-suicide. A wealthy Uptown man, a well-known Uptown woman. Both surrounded by death even before death came to them. Had he killed his wife for her instead of for that female judge, and then, had they quarreled, and then... Or had the judge come, discovered them, and...

What in God's name goes on behind the doors of those big expensive Uptown houses?

Inexplicably, Elena Quintero's face came into my mind. She would bear her child alone—a final gift from her dead husband, some would say. Or was it René's? Had I, in the throes of love for René, threatened to expose the truth? Had he been sleeping with both of us?

I covered my ears with my hands, not so much to shut out the distant sounds of my executioner coming toward me door by door, room by room, but to stop the cacophony of questions, images, voices I knew but could not recognize that would ask and ask until Madeline, Elena, and I faded, fused together, became part of the eternal lurid Uptown mythology. Poor little girls every one.

He was in the next room. I could tell by the elapsed time that he was being very thorough. It would do no good to hide in a closet or under the bed. I took the beautiful antique chair from Madeline's secretary and jammed it under the doorknob as I twisted the small lock just below. The door was old and sturdy, not one of the hollow-core kind that a single kick would shatter.

But it made no difference. It would not keep him out for long. Some part of my mind, still cool and distant and observing, was surprised at the effort one would make for a moment or two more of life. What did that say of all the moments I had lived before?

That same Observer I had experienced in Schwegmann's Supermarket, some part of me that stood alert and free of the panic that was building inside, sending torrents of adrenaline through my body, thought to wonder: Who is this killer, and why has he come to murder René and me? Do you suppose this man who is about to kill you was involved in Madeline's death?

That would be ironic, wouldn't it? Poor lonely little girl...

The knob turned softly once, and then the door crashed inward as if someone outside had placed a grenade against it. The lights came on and speared my eyes and he was crouched there, faceless, his arms rigid, that pistol with the silencer traversing, scanning the room and settling on my chest.

—Well, it's the fucking lady D.A.

—They're going to find you, and you'll never get to the lockup alive, I heard myself saying, amazed that my voice even worked.

And then, in that luminous attenuated instant, I understood. Given some small portion of grace, we do not die as animals, screeching and slavering for another breath, another fractional subdivision of a second of life. We die as human beings. I was about to die still talking, defiant, prophetic as Cassandra.

From behind the ski mask, a laugh, then that harsh accented voice that I suddenly recognized.

—You told me that once before, baby, it said, as he lifted the pistol to aim between my eyes.

—Hey, motherfucker, I heard in a harsh, hard-edged upstate accent coming from behind the shooter, from somewhere down the hall.

I know as well as anyone that nothing happens in slow motion except on a screen, but it took a month for the shooter to turn toward that angelic voice, toward the great swelling sound I had heard approaching down the hallway like a tidal wave that took years, decades, to arrive.

When it did, when that roar burst over me, I could not tear my eyes away from what happened to the man who had thought to kill me.

He exploded.

He disintegrated, and the hand and arm bearing the gun dissolved and disappeared. His chest turned into bloody foam, a spray that slapped loudly back against the wall at the end of the hallway. His lower body and legs skittered away and struck a door across the hall, fell, and continued to twitch and dance as if, on the far side of dying, a damned crazed endless disco party was going on. His head fell like a melon, the mask frazzled and thrust away. I recognized what was left of the face.

It was Santorini Malaporte.

—Sonofabitch, I heard someone say from down the hall. —I thought I'd seen everything.

—Wes . . . I heard myself crying out.

—Right here, sweetheart, he called as he reached the door of Madeline's bedroom carrying some kind of enormous weapon, stepping carefully across the ruin he had made, dropping the gun to sweep me up in his arms and hold me for perhaps six weeks, as we kissed and kissed again.

The ambulance team was working on René. I couldn't believe anyone covered with so much blood was alive, but Wes and Rat, both talking at once, kept trying to tell me anecdotes of bloodless death and bloody survival. I suppose I believed some part of what they said. I needed to get up and walk, to release the tension, but Wes wouldn't—or couldn't—let go of me.

It seemed that now the horror was done, Wes's imagination had kicked into gear, and he was terrified at what might have happened if he had not gone by Henry Holman's, if Henry in his drunken rage had not spewed out, in confidence to Wes, his best good buddy and fellow revenger, that he had stewed and stewed and at last found himself the way out of his frustration. He had bought a contract on René St. Juste. Who was

the mechanic hired? Why Wes ought to know the answer to that. And when would the wipeout go down?
Why any time now. Any time at all. Maybe at this very
moment...

While Wes kept pulling me close to him, kissing me
over and over, Rat was looking at the gun he had
picked up in the bedroom.

—This here is what you used?

—If you say so, Wes mumbled, whispering something vulgar and interesting in my ear.

—Shit, man. . . . Remember how you made fun of me
when I took all that hardware out to Desire Project?

—Ummm, Wes hummed, nibbling on my ear, his
hands moving over my hips in public in a very private
way.

—Wes . . . I said.

—I'm a tactile person, he whispered. —No, shit, I'm
sorry. It's just that . . . you're alive. Dennie, you're . . .
alive and okay.

I turned away from Rat for a moment and looked at
Wes. There were tears in his eyes. Tears of relief and
pride . . . and love. I reached over and pulled him to
me. We kissed for a century or so. If he really needed to
feel me up in public, I decided I could bear it. For
twenty or thirty years.

Rat was still shaking his head over the shotgun. —I
got to tell you, I mean as a friend . . . This is what they
call . . . overkill.

Wes broke off our kiss, his forehead furrowed.

—What the fuck is eating you? he asked Rat. —You
gonna charge me with littering? You want to see my
pest control license?

Rat pursed his lips. —Come on. All I'm saying is,
how come you got you a ten-gauge shotgun with
number two shot, and let go with both barrels? I mean,

I ain't gonna charge you with nothing. But old René-baby here has got him a civil suit for destruction of property. You seen that back wall down the corridor?

Wes squinted at him. —A ten gauge? Hell, I just grabbed the first shotgun I saw, and... ten gauge?

Rat grinned. —That's what it says on the receiver.

Wes nodded. —I guess that explains it.

—No, it don't, Rat said. —I'm still waiting for something like an explanation. I mean, like you gonna write a story, right?

—I guess.

—I gotta write a report. How come you made this seventh cavalry move?

Wes drew a deep breath. Without letting go of me.

—When Holman spilled his guts, I thought, hell, the old man's drunk on his ass. He's just fooling with me, saying what he'd *like* to do. But what if he isn't fooling? Maybe that coonass bastard St. Juste did burn his old lady. But he's supposed to get a trial. If that doesn't go right, *then* Henry could hire him somebody...

—That's nice, Rat smiled. —At least you got the sequence right.

—So I came on down here to tell St. Juste he'd better find him a big rock to hide under just in case... till I could get hold of you.

—Aw, Rat said, —you thought of me. Your basic old beat cop.

—But when I got to the house, I saw Dennie's car was out front. I pushed the door bell, and nobody answered. I took a look inside through one of those glass panels beside the door, and there was René stretched and popped. I mean it looked like a blood bank had sprung a leak.

—I'm gonna stipulate that, Rat said, looking over at the dark patch near the library door. —So then what?

—I saw this guy in the ski mask step out into the light. With a pistol...and a silencer. I thought, shit, this is a bad scene. Henry's actually fucking gone and done it. Then I remembered Denise's car was out front, and I damned near passed out.

—All right, Rat said. —But I still got you at the front door.

—Not for long you don't, Wes said. —I cut around the left side of the house and saw the kitchen door open. That's where he busted in. Early on, probably. Before St. Juste came home.

—So you went in there...

—Shit no. I kept moving. I wanted to cut him off, like maybe break a window and yell like hell. I didn't have a gun. You bastards won't let me carry a gun.

—I think maybe we should talk about that, Rat said quietly.

—Anyhow I made it across the courtyard and came up on the study or whatever. There was a light on inside and I could see a whole rack of guns.

—But the door was locked, I said. —Wasn't it?

—Yeah, it was locked. But I wrapped a handkerchief around my hand and pounded through the glass. There was this pane with a little paper tag on it...

Rat and I looked at one another. Those who have not experienced the past are blessed to repeat it.

—And as soon as I was in, I grabbed up this shotgun and broke it open, and there were two shells in it and there wasn't any time, so I made the door and stepped out into the hall and...

Wes smiled like a little boy.

—And that was it. I saw that sonofabitch down there and I said something, and he turned and I pulled both triggers and...

—Right, Rat smiled ruefully. —You know we found

pieces of that silly bastard in the yard where you blew out the brick veneer?

—Good, Wes said. —I never did like him.

—What are you saying? Rat asked. —I mean, Santorini Malaporte was your man for that "Hit Parade" series.

—He was dogshit, Wes said, looking sideways at me. —It was a good story, but all the time I was listening and writing, I was thinking, You shit. You miserable shit.

Rat stared at him in mock surprise. —How come you say that? I thought Malaporte was your kind of stand-up guy.

Wes stared back, no humor in his expression. —He was a back-shooter. He liked hurting people. It wasn't business with him. It was pleasure.

—So you turned that damned off-brand ten-gauge shotgun down the hall and said, I don't dig your style.

Wes's face lit up. He smiled as if he'd just won a major journalism award. —Yeah, he said brightly. —That's just the way it was. Then, when I managed to get back on my feet... Listen, it was almost as bad at my end of that goddamned gun as at his.... I shot from the hip, and...

A uniformed officer came over to Rat and whispered something. Rat nodded.

—Youall excuse me, he said. —I got a call. I know you can occupy each other.

As he walked toward the phone, Wes turned to me, his face pale, not from fear or regret at having killed. I'm still not sure he understands either of those emotions. He would never hurt anyone unless it was necessary. But if it were necessary...

—I'd...like to occupy you forever, he said to me. —Dennie, I love you so much...

I found his arms around me once more.

—Wes, my darling, I whispered and said no more, knowing he would understand that, at last and forever, I was saying, Yes, my love. It will be us for as long as I live.

Rat came back and joined us. Which was just as well. God knows what might have happened there in front of everyone if he hadn't.

—Hello young lovers, he laughed. —We got all the threads pulled together. My folks hit Malaporte's place with a warrant, and we done won the lottery. They come up with Mrs. St. Juste's jewelry down to the last piece, right? She must have called him when Lulu Washington walked out on her role in the play . . . and gave him the jewelry to do the job.

—So there *was* a dark stranger here that night, I said.

—When I think back on it . . . I was with Malaporte that Friday, Wes told us. —We were at my place working on the series. We were supposed to go all night so I could finish that Sunday, but he got a phone call from a woman and left early. It could have been Madeline St. Juste, but how would she know to . . . ?

—She could have guessed it reading the *Item*, Rat said.

—She didn't have to, I said, my voice sounding strange and distant. —Madeline called me that night . . . and I told her Wes and I had quarreled . . . that he was spending his nights debriefing a hired killer.

—But what does that tell us? Wes asked Rat.

—Huh?

—Did Malaporte kill her? Or did she do it and he just took away the gun and collected the jewelry for his pay?

—Ah, Rat smiled without humor. —I don't see we'll

ever know that for sure. But then, what the hell difference does it make?

There was a disturbance at the front door, and we looked up to see Elena Quintero pushing her way through the policemen there. I managed to wiggle free of Wes for a moment and stood up. It was another duty.

She knelt beside René, whom the ambulance team had on a gurney, ready to wheel outside. She kissed him and he smiled up at her. He raised one hand weakly to touch her cheek.

—We're going to be... all right, he said, his voice whispy, distant. —Whatever the price, we've...

—Oh, my love, she said, her voice breaking as the paramedics drew him away from her. As she rose sobbing, I took her into my arms.

—Everything is going to be fine, I said. —Get hold of yourself. Hysterics aren't good for the baby.

Her sobs stopped, and her face showed surprise as she realized what I had said. —You know?

—René told me.

Elena nodded. —It's just as well. Oh God, Denise, I don't care what anyone thinks, what anyone says...

I kissed her and held her close. —You've won, I said. —Both of you. You're going to be happy... all three of you.

—Three, Elena laughed. —Maybe five or six...

She followed the paramedics out, and I went back to join Wes and Rat. They were having a subdued argument.

—He'll walk, Wes was saying. —You wait and see.

—Like hell, Rat was telling him. —Lazy Louie's gonna do ten making big rocks into little rocks.

—Not without Santo's testimony he's not. I'm giving eight to five Louie's gonna stroll off into the sunset and

have one single red rose sent to Malaporte's grave
every year.

—Ha, Rat said, —on Detonation Day?

They both laughed and then looked up at me.

—I can't imagine why, I said slowly, with what
seemed to me great precision, —but I'm feeling tired.
Would either of you gentlemen like to drive me home?

—Why sure, Rat said, starting to stand up.

Wes pushed him back onto the couch as he turned
to me.

—Whose home? he asked with a grin.

—Let's go find the car. We'll negotiate.

—Don't youall get lost, Rat called after us. —Now
that you're found . . .

We had just reached the door when someone pushed
past the officer outside. He had almost passed us when
he recognized me. It was Jock Marvell. He looked
around, spotted Rat, and the coroner's team that had
finally managed to get Malaporte more or less into a
body bag.

—Denise, I need to speak to you and Captain Trapp
about my client, Jock said.

—Too late, Rat told him, grinning viciously, pointing
at the body bag. —My man Colvin here iced down
your client. That sack of shit used to be Santo Malaporte.

Jock looked at the gurney quizzically as it passed on
the way out. —Is that so? Who was Santo killing?

—Does it matter? I asked him coldly.

—I suppose not. But I want to touch base with you
about my new client . . . Henry Holman. He just called
me from his house and asked me to arrange his turning
himself in and . . .

Rat and Wes and I looked at one another.

—Crazy Lady, Wes laughed as he took my arm and

propelled me out the door, past the police cars and the coroner's ambulance with their whirling red lights, out to the Mercedes that I'd never expected to see again. We stopped there and kissed once more, neither of us noticing how much colder it had become, or how wind from the north clawed at us and blew sleet into our hair.

When I awoke, I remembered everything. I had had a long dream filled with people I loved. People who had died when I was very small, people who had died not long ago. My dream was divided into scenes, if you will.

My grandfather and I were sitting on his favorite marble bench in the garden of my house on State Street.

It was spring and the magnolias were beginning to open, spilling their fragrance all around us. My grandfather was telling me it was time to move on now, that I would have to leave this place. This was a world we'd loved, where generations of our family had lived and died. But no world goes on forever. Once, ages ago, we had lived in Brittany, but our generations there had ended. We had come from that cold northern clime down into the hot humid swamps and endless windraked marshes of Louisiana. We had helped build this town, forged its ways, its manners. But that was going, too.

He seemed without regret, as if he had learned that the building of a human place was somehow more important than its habitation. We should be kind, remember, look forward, he whispered to me, his face wreathed in a wise smile I remember so well.

—Where will you go? Madeline was asking as we walked side by side in Audubon Park on a quiet summer evening. —Where will you and Wesley go and make your lives?

—I don't know, I told her. —Does it matter?

She shook her head gravely, her bright blond hair moving from side to side. —No. I could have moved away from Uptown New Orleans and never taken a step. At last, above all, I betrayed . . . myself.

Then her expression brightened. She smiled and took my hand. —But you won't, will you? That's my gift to you, darling. You'll never be a poor lonely little girl again.

We laughed together, and then I felt my mother brushing my hair, and I looked into the tall mirror above her vanity and saw my tiny face and hers, worn and fragile, filled with love poised above me. She said nothing, only drawing the silver-mounted brush through my hair that was the color of cornstalks in July under a Wedgwood sky. She reached down, kissed me, and I realized I wasn't lonely at all.

Then I was awake, sitting up in bed, disoriented for a moment until I realized that I was in Wes's apartment, in his bed. And that he wasn't beside me.

I looked across the room and saw the glow of a cigar. He was standing next to the glass doors that opened onto his courtyard. I rose, pulled a blanket off the bed, and walked to his side. I could feel the deep cold radiating from the window as he silently put his arm around me and drew me close. Then I saw what he was looking at.

Outside it was snowing. Snow was falling from the dark featureless sky down onto the glass-topped table and wrought-iron chairs there in the courtyard. It had already covered the rough irregular flagstones and was sifting through the bare limbs of that mimosa just beyond the glass. The flakes were large and beautiful, and they had begun to build up on the thick dark leaves of an old magnolia across the way, to bend down the stiff bunched branches of camellias and azaleas planted along the wall opposite us.

The snowflakes seemed to tumble down only to be swept upward again by wind that muttered and whispered and rattled the glass doors, and a distant streetlight outside the courtyard wall gave it all a strange peaceful golden tone as if, by merely opening the doors, we could step into an old-fashioned engraving of an Uptown New Orleans of long ago in most unusual weather.

I closed my eyes, feeling somehow that I was leaving my New Orleans, that the vehicle of my departure was Wes's arms around me, his lips touching my cheek, my shoulders.

I could see the snow drifting in the garden on State Street, filling the ornate carving of the old marble bench, drawing the gardenias' branches down to the bark-covered flower beds. It lay thick in the heavy ancient branches of the oaks in Audubon Park, falling on the glistening frozen lagoons and across the silent bridle paths that curved between leafless sycamores and gum trees. I could see snow swirling and settling on the ageless worn brick and granite tombs in St. Louis Cemetery with doors that opened only to receive grief, where almost two hundred years of endings and conclusions rested speechless, none complete, all finished —obscured now under a blanket of matchless white that joined together for a little while the dwellings of the living and the dead.

Behind us, I heard the tiny voice of an announcer on an all-night music station say that snow was general all over south Louisiana from the Sabine River to the Rigolets. Snow was very rare so far south, and tomorrow there would be no school. The children would awaken and see their homes, their neighborhoods, as none had ever seen them before.

I opened my eyes as the music began once more. Now the snowflakes were beginning to stick to the glass in front of me. I put out my hand and touched the chill resisting surface, remembering where Wes and I had been, looking forward to where we were going. Then Wes drew my hand away from the cold, lifted me in his arms, and carried me back to bed.